PUFFIN BOOKS

THE PUFFIN BOOK OF GHOSTS AND GHOULS

In this eerie and unnerving collection, Gene Kemp has brought together some of the most chilling tales of the supernatural that you will ever find. Joan Aiken, Peter Dickinson, Susan Price, Rogert Westall and Gene Kemp herself are just a few of the acclaimed authors who have contributed stories to this diverse and entertaining collection. The ghosts here are not just shadowy shapes floating down the staircases of old mansions or conventional spooks rattling chains in dungeons. They all have their individual personalities – some are funny, some shy, some noisy and disruptive, while others are grim and formidable, and some are downright terrifying. We meet a baby ghost in Ursula Moray Williams' 'A Ghost of One's Own', a cheeky modern boy ghost in Marjorie Darke's 'Hi! It's Me', a Victorian girl ghost with frightening supernatural powers in Jane Gardan's 'Bang, Bang – Who's Dead?', and even a cat ghost in Gene Kemp's 'The Passing of Puddy!'

The ghosts and ghouls come to life and cast a spell on us in these haunting tales and as they drew us into their world, they seem to become uncannily real and the living people in the stories uncannily ghost-like.

Gene Kemp has been interested in stories about the supernatural from an early age. She is one of the foremost British Children's authors of today. She has written nineteen books and is best-known for *The Turbulent Term of Type Tiller*, her first novel featuring the famous Cricklepit Combined School which won her the Library Association's Carnegie Medal and the 1977 Other Award. She was born in Wigginton, a small Midlands village outside Tamworth. After years of teaching she retired to concentrate on her writing, and now lives in Exeter. In 1984 she was awarded an honorary Master of Arts degree by Exeter University in recognition of her achievement as a writer of children's books.

Also in this series

THE PUFFIN BOOK OF
HORSE AND PONY STORIES

THE PUFFIN BOOK OF
SCIENCE FICTION STORIES

THE PUFFIN BOOK OF
SONG AND DANCE

THE PUFFIN BOOK OF
SCHOOL STORIES

THE PUFFIN BOOK OF
FUNNY STORIES

The Puffin Book of

GHOSTS
and
GHOULS

STORIES CHOSEN BY

GENE KEMP

Illustrations by Nick Harris

PUFFIN BOOKS

PUFFIN BOOKS

Published by the Penguin Group
Penguin Books Ltd, 27 Wrights Lane, London W8 5TZ, England
Penguin Books USA Inc., 375 Hudson Street, New York, New York 10014, USA
Penguin Books Australia Ltd, Ringwood, Victoria, Australia
Penguin Books Canada Ltd, 10 Alcorn Avenue, Toronto, Ontario, Canada M4V 3B2
Penguin Books (NZ) Ltd, 182–190 Wairau Road, Auckland 10, New Zealand

Penguin Books Ltd, Registered Offices: Harmondsworth, Middlesex, England

First published by Viking 1992
Published in Puffin Books 1993
1 3 5 7 9 10 8 6 4 2

This collection copyright © Gene Kemp, 1992
Illustration copyright © Nick Harris, 1992

This acknowledgements on pages 000–000 constitute an extension
to this copyright page

All rights reserved

The moral right of the authors has been asserted

Printed in England by Clays Ltd, St Ives plc
Filmset in Lasercomp Bembo

Except in the United States of America, this book is sold subject
to the condition that it shall not, by way of trade or otherwise, be lent,
re-sold, hired out, or otherwise circulated without the publisher's
prior consent in any form of binding or cover other than that in
which it is published and without a similar condition including this
condition being imposed on the subsequent purchaser

Contents

W. SUSSEX INSTITUTE
OF
HIGHER EDUCATION
LIBRARY

There was two fellows out working in a field, hoeing turnips they was, and the one he stop and he lean on his hoe, and he mop his vace and he say, 'Yur – I don't believe in these yur ghosteses!'

And t'other man he say, 'Don't 'ee?'

And he VANISHED!

The Men in the Turnip Field
(*Trad*)

Introduction

'Scary Monsters, super creeps . . .'

Draw the curtains, turn on the fire, for it's dark outside and the wind stirs uneasily in the trees. Push off your shoes, curl up and open your book . . . sh! What was that? No need to look round over your shoulder, it was only a creaking floor-board; there's no one, nothing creeping up behind you. Besides, you're very brave. You wouldn't be afraid of any old . . . ghost or monster . . . evil person or wicked child, would you? Or would you?

Read this selection and see.

It begins with a strange, compelling story, *The Giant's Necklace* by Michael Morpurgo, that takes you by the hand into another world. Susan Price tells of revenge in *The Horn*, a tale most appropriate for today. Penelope Lively's *Uninvited Ghosts* is both funny and comforting after Jane Gardam's *Bang, Bang – Who's Dead?* and Philippa Pearce's *The Shadow-Cage* have scared you witless as they did me. That last one especially gives me the 'screaming abdabs' because it's just the sort of thing I'd do, searching for something you shouldn't have in the middle of the night in a place where you shouldn't be till you realize you're in a situation there might be no getting out of. In *The Passing of Puddy* Jess has to get everybody (including the cat) out of their situation. Can she do it? Peter Dickinson's *The Spring* carries a cold chill and *The Veldt* by Ray Bradbury is very gruesome. *A Ghost of One's Own* by Ursula Moray Williams and *Humble-puppy* by Joan Aiken are kinder but just as weird.

My love of strange situations landed me living in an ancient dilapidated house on Dartmoor, brr. Now, the moor's a place for hauntings; it's full of ghoulies, ghosties, and long-leggity beasties. One of the most frightening could be called a ghost of the road. If you ever drive along the B3212 between Postbridge and Two Bridges, take care. Several accidents have taken place there. Two cyclists felt their handlebars wrenched out of their hands causing them to crash in a ditch. In olden days they say horses ran wild and crashed their coaches. A motor cycle was taken over, its side-car overturned killing the passenger. Hairy Hands appear out of nowhere and attack the traveller or the vehicle. One woman in a caravan parked in a lay-by saw a huge Hairy Hand clawing its way up the window, argh. She made the sign of the cross and it vanished. So – if you're travelling there, especially at night, look out for . . . Hairy Hands.

There's a haunted school at Cullompton in Devon. I visited it to read stories and the headmaster told me that if you stay late at night, the corridor that goes past the cloakroom and leads to the front door suddenly turns cold and the sound of marching feet can be heard. Roman legionaries are marching, marching. The noise will grow louder and louder, then turn, halt and march away. A Roman camp lies under the school.

Who fancies staying late at that school?

In the mean time here are some strange offerings for you. Stories that are frightening, fun, sad, haunting, strange, weird, eerie, mysterious, doom-laden. I hope you find plenty to your taste . . . whoooo!

Spooky reading,

Gene Kemp

The Giant's Necklace

MICHAEL MORPURGO

The necklace stretched from one end of the kitchen table to the other, around the sugar bowl at the far end and back again, stopping only a few inches short of the toaster. The discovery on the beach of a length of abandoned fishing line draped with seaweed had first suggested the idea to Cherry; and every day of the holiday since then had been spent in one single-minded pursuit, the creation of a necklace of glistening pink cowrie shells. She had sworn to herself and to everyone else that the necklace would not be complete until it reached the toaster; and when Cherry vowed she would do something, she invariably did it.

Cherry was the youngest in a family of older brothers, four of them, who had teased her relentlessly since the day she was born, eleven years before. She referred to them as 'the four mistakes', for it was a family joke that each son had been an attempt to produce a daughter. To their huge delight Cherry reacted passionately

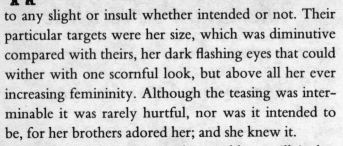

to any slight or insult whether intended or not. Their particular targets were her size, which was diminutive compared with theirs, her dark flashing eyes that could wither with one scornful look, but above all her ever increasing femininity. Although the teasing was interminable it was rarely hurtful, nor was it intended to be, for her brothers adored her; and she knew it.

Cherry was poring over her necklace, still in her dressing gown. Breakfast had just been cleared away and she was alone with her mother. She fingered the shells lightly, turning them gently until the entire necklace lay flat with the rounded pink of the shells all uppermost. Then she bent down and breathed on each of them in turn, polishing them carefully with a napkin.

'There's still the sea in them,' she said to no one in particular. 'You can still smell it, and I washed them and washed them, you know.'

'You've only got today, Cherry,' said her mother coming over to the table and putting an arm around her. 'Just today, that's all. We're off back home tomorrow morning first thing. Why don't you call it a day, dear? You've been at it every day – you *must* be tired of it by now. There's no need to go on, you know. We all think it's a fine necklace and quite long enough. It's long enough surely?'

Cherry shook her head slowly. 'Nope,' she said. 'Only that little bit left to do and then it's finished.'

'But they'll take hours to collect, dear,' her mother said weakly, recognizing and at the same time respecting her daughter's persistence.

'Only a few hours,' said Cherry, bending over, her brows furrowing critically as she inspected a flaw in one of her shells, 'that's all it'll take. D'you know, there are five thousand, three hundred and twenty-five shells in my necklace already? I counted them, so I know.'

'Isn't that enough, dear?' her mother said desperately.

'Nope,' said Cherry. 'I said I'd reach the toaster, and I'm going to reach the toaster.'

Her mother turned away to continue the drying up.

'Well, I can't spend all day on the beach today, Cherry,' she said. 'If you haven't finished by the time we come away I'll have to leave you there. We've got to pack up and tidy the house – there'll be no time in the morning.'

'I'll be all right,' said Cherry, cocking her head on one side to view the necklace from a different angle. 'There's never been a necklace like this before, not in all the world. I'm sure there hasn't.' And then, 'You can leave me there Mum, and I'll walk back. It's only a mile or so along the cliff path and half a mile back across the fields. I've done it before on my own. It's not far.'

There was a thundering on the stairs and a sudden rude invasion of the kitchen. Cherry was surrounded by her four brothers who leant over the table in mock appreciation of her necklace.

'Ooh, pretty.'

'Do they come in other colours? I mean, pink's not my colour.'

'Bit big though, isn't it?' said one of them – she didn't know which and it didn't matter. He went on: 'I mean it's a bit big for a necklace?' War had been declared again, and Cherry responded predictably.

'That depends,' she said calmly, shrugging her shoulders because she knew that would irritate them.

'On what does it depend?' said her oldest brother, pompously.

'On who's going to wear it of course, ninny,' she said swiftly.

'Well, who is going to wear it?' he replied.

'It's for a giant,' she said, her voice full of serious innocence. 'It's a giant's necklace, and it's still not big enough.'

It was the perfect answer, an answer she knew would send her brothers into fits of hysterical hilarity. She loved to make them laugh at her and could do it at the drop of a hat. Of course she no more believed in giants than they did, but if it tickled them pink to believe she did, then why not pretend?

She turned on them, fists flailing, and chased them back up the stairs, her eyes burning with simulated fury. 'Just 'cos you don't believe in anything 'cept motor bikes and football and all that rubbish, just 'cos you're great big, fat, ignorant pigs . . .' She hurled insults up the stairs after them and the worse they became the more they loved it.

Boat Cove just below Zennor Head was the beach

they had found and occupied. Every year for as long as Cherry could remember they had rented the same granite cottage, set back in the fields below the Eagle's Nest, and every year they came to the same beach because no one else did. In two weeks not another soul had ventured down the winding track through the bracken from the coastal path. It was a long climb down and a very much longer one up. The beach itself was almost hidden from the path that ran along the cliff top a hundred feet above. It was private and perfect and theirs. The boys swam in amongst the rocks, diving and snorkelling for hours on end. Her mother and father would sit side by side on stripy deck chairs. She would read endlessly and he would close his eyes against the sun and dream for hours on end.

Cherry moved away from them and clambered over the rocks to a narrow strip of sand in the cove beyond the rock, and here it was that she mined for the cowrie shells. In the gritty sand under the cliff face she had found a particularly rich deposit so that they were not hard to find; but she was looking for pink cowrie shells of a uniform length, colour and shape – and that was what took the time. Occasionally the boys would swim around the rocks and in to her little beach, emerging from the sea all goggled and flippered to mock her. But as she paid them little attention they soon tired and went away again. She knew time was running short. This was her very last chance to find enough shells to complete the giant's necklace, and it had to be done.

The sea was calmer that day than she had ever seen it. The heat beat down from a windless, cloudless sky; even the gulls and kittiwakes seemed to be silenced by the sun. Cherry searched on, stopping only for a picnic lunch of pasties and tomatoes with the family before returning at once to her shells.

In the end the heat proved too much for her mother and father who left the beach earlier than usual in mid-afternoon to begin to tidy up the cottage. The boys soon followed because they had tired of finding minia-ture crabs and seaweed instead of the sunken wrecks and treasure they had been seeking, so that by tea-time Cherry was left on her own on the beach with strict instructions to keep her hat on, not to bathe alone and to be back well before dark. She had calcu-lated she needed one hundred and fifty more cowrie shells and so far she had found only eighty. She would be back, she insisted, when she had finished collecting enough shells and not before.

Had she not been so immersed in her search, sifting the shells through her fingers, she would have noticed the dark grey bank of cloud rolling in from the At-lantic. She would have noticed the white horses gather-ing out at sea and the tide moving remorselessly in to cover the rocks between her and Boat Cove. When the clouds cut off the warmth from the sun as evening came on and the sea turned grey, she shivered with cold and slipped on her jersey and jeans. She did look up then and saw that the sea was angry, but she saw no threat in that and did not look back over her shoulder towards Boat Cove. She was aware that time was running short so she went down on her knees again and dug feverishly in the sand. There were still thirty shells to collect and she was not going home without them.

It was the baleful sound of a fog-horn somewhere out at sea beyond Gunnards Head that at last forced Cherry to consider her own predicament. Only then did she take some account of the incoming tide. She looked for the rocks she would have to clamber over to reach Boat Cove again and the winding track that would take her up to the cliff path and safety, but they were gone. Where they should have been, the sea was already driving in against the cliff face. She was cut off. For many moments Cherry stared in disbelief and wondered if her memory was deceiving her, until the sea, sucked back into the Atlantic for a brief moment, revealed the rocks that marked her route back to Boat Cove. Then she realized at last that the sea had undergone a grim metamorphosis. In a confusion of wonder and fear she looked out to sea at the heaving ocean that moved in towards her, seeing it now as a writhing grey monster breathing its fury on the rocks with every pounding wave.

Still Cherry did not forget her shells, but wrapping them inside her towel she tucked them into her jersey and waded out through the surf towards the rocks. If she timed it right, she reasoned, she could scramble back over them and into the Cove as the surf retreated. And she reached the first of the rocks without too much difficulty; the sea here seemed to be protected from the force of the ocean by the rocks further out. Holding fast to the first rock she came to, and with the sea up around her waist, she waited for the next incoming wave to break and retreat. The wave was unexpectedly impotent and fell limply on the rocks around her. She knew her moment had come and took it. She was not to know that piling up far out at sea was the first of the giant storm waves that had gathered several hundred miles out in the Atlantic bringing with it all the momentum and violence of the deep ocean.

The rocks were slippery underfoot and more than once Cherry slipped down into seething white rock pools where she had played so often when the tide was out. But she struggled on until finally she had climbed high enough to be able to see the thin strip of sand that was all that was left of Boat Cove. It was only a few yards away, so close. Until now she had been crying involuntarily, but now as she recognized the little path up through the bracken her heart was lifted with hope and anticipation. She knew that the worst was over, that if the sea would only hold back she would reach the sanctuary of the Cove. She turned and looked behind her to see how far away the next wave was, just to reassure herself that she had enough time. But the great surge of green water was on her before she could register either disappointment or fear. She was hurled back against the rock below her and covered at once by the sea. She was conscious as she went down that she was drowning, but she still clutched her shells against her chest and was glad she had enough of them at last to finish the giant's necklace. Those were her last thinking thoughts before the sea took her away.

Cherry lay on her side where the tide had lifted her and coughed until her lungs were clear. She woke as the sea came in once again and frothed around her legs. She rolled over on her back, feeling the salt spray on her face, and saw that it was night. The sky above her was dashed with stars and the moon rode through the clouds. She scrambled to her feet, one hand still holding her precious shells close to her. Instinctively she backed away from the sea and looked around her. With growing dismay she saw that she had been thrown back on the wrong side of the rocks, that she was not in Boat Cove. The tide had left only a few feet of sand and rock between her and the cliff face. There was no way back through the sea to safety. She turned round to face the cliff that she realized would be her last hope, for she remembered that this little beach vanished completely at high tide. If she stayed where she was she would surely be swept away again and this time she might not be so fortunate. But the cold seemed to have calmed her and she reasoned more deliberately now, wondering why she had not tried climbing the cliff before. She had hurried into her first attempt at escape and it had very nearly cost her her life. She would wait this time until the sea forced her up the cliff. Perhaps the tide would not come in that far. Perhaps they would be looking for her by now. It was dark. Surely they would be searching. Surely they must find her soon. After all, they knew where she was. Yes, she thought, best just to wait and hope.

She settled down on a ledge of rock that was the first step up on to the cliff face, drew her knees up to her chin to keep out the chill and waited. She watched as the sea crept ever closer, each wave lashing her with spray and eating away gradually at the beach. She closed her eyes and prayed, hoping against hope that when she opened them the sea would be retreating. But her prayers went unanswered and the sea came in to cover the beach. Once or twice she thought she heard voices above her on the cliff path, but when she called out no one came. She continued to shout for help every few minutes, forgetting it was futile against the continuous roar and hiss of the waves. A pair of raucous white gulls flew down from the cliffs to investigate her and she called to them for help, but they did not seem to understand and wheeled away into the night.

She stayed sitting on her rock until the waves threatened to dislodge her and then reluctantly she began her climb. She would go as far as she needed to and no further. She had scanned the first few feet above for footholds and it did look quite a simple climb to begin with, and so it proved. But her hands were numbed with cold and her legs began to tremble with the strain almost at once. She could see that the ledge she had now reached was the last deep one visible on the cliff face. The shells in her jersey were restricting her freedom of movement so she decided she would leave them there. Wrapped tight in the towel they would be quite safe. She took the soaking bundle out of her jersey and placed it carefully against the rock face on the ledge beside her, pushing it in as far as it would go. 'I'll be back for you,' she said, and reached up for the next lip of rock. Just below her the sea crashed against the cliff as if it wanted to suck her from the rock face and claim her once again. Cherry determined not to look down but to concentrate on the climb.

She imagined at first that the glow of light above her was from a torch, and she shouted and screamed until she was weak from the effort of it. But although no answering call came from the night, the light remained, a pale beckoning light whose source now seemed to her wider perhaps than that of a torch. With renewed hope that had rekindled her strength and her courage, Cherry inched her way up the cliff towards the light until she found herself at the entrance to a narrow cave that was filled with a flickering yellow light like that of a candle shaken by the wind. She hauled herself up into the mouth of the cave and sat down exhausted, looking back down at the furious sea frothing beneath her. Relief and joy surged within her and she laughed aloud in triumph. She was safe and she had defied the sea and won. Her one regret was that she had had to leave her cowrie shells behind on the ledge. They were high enough, she thought, to escape the sea. She would fetch them tomorrow after the tide had gone down again.

For the first time now she began to think of her family and how worried they would be, but the thought of walking in through the front door all dripping and dramatic made her almost choke with excitement.

As she reached forward to brush a sharp stone from the sole of her foot, Cherry noticed that the narrow entrance to the cave was half sealed in. She ran her fingers over the stones and cement to make sure, for the light was poor. It was at that moment that she recognized exactly where she was. She recalled now the giant fledgling cuckoo one of her brothers had spotted, being fed by a tiny rock pipit earlier in the holidays, how they had quarrelled over the binoculars and how when she had finally usurped them and made her escape across the rocks she had found the cuckoo perched at the entrance to a narrow cave some way up the cliff face from the beach. She had asked then about the man-made walling and her father had told her of the old tin mines whose lodes and adits criss-crossed the entire coastal area around Zennor. This one, he said, might have been the mine they called Wheel North Grylls, and he thought the adit must have been walled up to prevent the seas from entering the mine in a storm. It was said there had been an accident in the mine only a few years after it was opened over a hundred years before and that the mine had had to close soon after when the mineowners ran out of money to make the necessary repairs. The entire story came back to her now, and she wondered where the cuckoo was and whether the rock pipit had died with the effort of keeping the fledgling alive. Tin mines, she thought, lead to the surface, and the way home. That thought and her natural inquisitiveness about the source of light persuaded her to her feet and into the tunnel.

The adit became narrower and lower as she crept forward, so that she had to go down on her hands and knees and sometimes flat on her stomach. Although she was not out of the wind, it seemed colder. She felt she was moving downwards for a minute or two, for the blood was coming to her head and her weight was heavy on her hands. Then quite suddenly she found the ground levelling out and saw a large tunnel ahead of her. There was no doubt as to which way she should turn for one way the tunnel was black and the other way was lighted with candles that lined the lode wall as far as she could see. She called out aloud: 'Anyone there? Anyone there?' and paused to listen for the reply; but all she could hear now was the muffled roar of the sea and the continuous echoing of dripping water.

The tunnel widened now and she could walk up-right again; but her feet hurt against the stone and so she moved slowly, feeling her way gently with each foot. She had gone only a short distance when she heard the tapping for the first time, distinct and rhythmic, a sound that was instantly recognizable as hammering. It became sharper and noticeably more metallic as she moved up the tunnel. She could hear the distant murmur of voices and the sound of falling stone. Before she came out of the tunnel and into the vast cave she knew she had happened upon a working mine.

The cave was dark in all but one corner and here she could see two men bending to their work, their backs towards her. One of them was inspecting the rock face closely whilst the other swung his hammer with controlled power, pausing only to spit on his hands from time to time. They wore round hats with turned up brims that served also as candlesticks, for a lighted candle was fixed to each, the light dancing with the shadows along the cave walls as they worked.

Cherry watched for some moments until she made up her mind what to do. She longed to rush up to them and tell of her escape and to ask them to take her to the surface, but a certain shyness overcame her and she held back. Her chance to interrupt came when they sat down against the rock face and opened their canteen. She was in the shadows and they still could not see her.

'Tea looks cold again,' one of them said gruffly. ''Tis always cold, I'm sure she makes it wi' cold water.'

'Oh stop your moaning, father,' said the other, a

younger voice, Cherry felt. 'She does her best. She's five little ones to look after and precious little to do it on. She does her best. You mustn't keep on at her so. It upsets her. She does her best.'

'So she does, lad, so she does. And so for that matter do I, but that don't stop her moaning at me and it'll not stop me moaning at her. If we didn't moan at each other lad, we'd have precious little else to talk about, and that's a fact. She expects it of me lad, and I expects it of her.'

'Excuse me,' Cherry said tentatively. She felt she had eavesdropped for long enough. She approached them slowly. 'Excuse me, but I've got a bit lost. I climbed the cliff, you see, 'cos I was cut off from the Cove. I was trying to get back, but I couldn't and I saw this light and so I climbed up. I want to get home and I wondered if you could help me get to the top?'

'Top?' said the older one, peering into the dark. 'Come closer, lad, where we can see you.'

'She's not a lad, father. Are you blind? Can you not see 'tis a filly. 'Tis a young filly, all wet through from the sea. Come,' the young man said, standing up and beckoning Cherry in. 'Don't be afeared little girl, we shan't harm you. Come on, you can have some of my tea if you like.'

They spoke their words in a manner Cherry had never heard before. It was not the usual Cornish burr, but heavier and rougher in tone and somehow old-fashioned. There were so many questions in her mind.

'But I thought the mine was closed a hundred years

ago,' she said nervously. 'That's what I was told anyway.'

'Well, you was told wrong,' said the old man whom Cherry could see more clearly now under his candle. His eyes were white and set far back in his head, unnaturally so she thought, and his lips and mouth seemed a vivid red in the candlelight.

'Closed, closed indeed, does it look closed to you? D'you think we're digging for worms? Over four thousand tons of tin last year and nine thousand of copper ore, and you ask is the mine closed! Over twenty fathoms below the sea this mine goes. We'll dig right out under the ocean, most of the way to 'Merica afore we close down this mine.'

He spoke passionately now, almost angrily, so that Cherry felt she had offended him.

'Hush father,' said the young man, taking off his jacket and wrapping it around Cherry's shoulders. 'She doesn't want to hear all about that. She's cold and wet. Can't you see? Now let's make a little fire to warm her through. She's shivered right through to her bones. You can see she is.'

'They all are,' said the old tinner, pulling himself to his feet. 'They all are.' And he shuffled past her into the dark. 'I'll fetch the wood,' he muttered, and then added, 'for all the good it'll do.'

'What does he mean?' Cherry asked the young man, for whom she felt an instant liking. 'What did he mean by that?'

'Oh pay him no heed, little girl,' he said. 'He's an

old man now and tired of the mine. We're both tired of it, but we're proud of it see, and we've nowhere else to go, nothing else to do.'

He had a kind voice that was reassuring to Cherry. He seemed somehow to know the questions she wanted to ask, for he answered them now without her ever asking.

'Sit down by me while you listen, girl,' he said. 'Father will make a fire to warm you and I shall tell you how we come to be here. You won't be afeared now, will you?'

Cherry looked up into his face which was younger than she had expected from his voice; but like his father's the eyes seemed sad and deep set, yet they smiled at her gently and she smiled back.

'That's my girl. It was a new mine this, promising everyone said. The best tin in Cornwall and that means the best tin in the world. 1865 it started up and they were looking for tinners, and so father found a cottage down by Treveal and came to work here. I was already fourteen, so I joined him down the mine. We prospered and the mine prospered, to start with. Mother and the little children had full bellies and there was talk of sinking a fresh shaft. Times were good and promised to be better.'

Cherry sat transfixed as the story of the disaster unfolded. She heard how they had been trapped by a fall of rocks, about how they had worked to pull them away, but behind every rock was another rock and another rock. She heard how they had never even heard any sound of rescue. They had died, he said, in two days or so because the air was bad and because there was too little of it.

'Father has never accepted it; he still thinks he's alive, that he goes home to mother and the little children each evening. But he's dead, just like me. I can't tell him though, for he'd not understand and it would break his heart if he ever knew.'

'So you aren't real,' said Cherry, trying to grasp the implications of his story. 'So I'm just imagining all this. You're just a dream?'

'No dream, my girl,' said the young man laughing out loud. 'No more'n we're imagining you. We're real right enough, but we're dead and have been for a hundred years and more. Ghosts, spirits, that's what living folk call us, come to think of it that's what I called us when I was alive.'

Cherry was on her feet suddenly and backing away.

'No need to be afeared, little girl,' said the young man, holding out his hand towards her. 'We won't harm you. No one can harm you, not now. Look, he's started the fire already. Come over and warm yourself. Come, it'll be all right, girl. We'll look after you. We'll help you.'

'But I want to go home,' Cherry said, feeling the panic rising to her voice and trying to control it. 'I know you're kind, but I want to go home. My mother will be worried about me. They'll be out looking for me. Your light saved my life and I want to thank you. But I must go else they'll worry themselves sick, I know they will.'

'You going back home?' the young man asked, and then he nodded. 'I s'pose you'll want to see your family again.'

''Course I am,' said Cherry, perplexed by the question. ''Course I do.'

''Tis a pity,' he said sadly. 'Everyone passes through and no one stays. They all want to go home, but then so do I. You'll want me to guide you to the surface I s'pose.'

'I'm not the first then?' Cherry said. 'There's been others climb up into the mine to escape from the sea? You saved lots of people then?'

'A few,' said the tinner, nodding. 'A few.'

'You're a kind person,' Cherry said, warming to the sadness in the young man's voice. 'I never thought ghosts would be kind.'

'We're just people, people who've passed on,' replied the young man taking her elbow and leading her towards the fire. 'There's nice people and there's nasty people. It's the same if you're alive or if you're dead. You're a nice person, I can tell that, even though I haven't known you for long. I'm sad because I should like to be alive again with my friends and go rabbiting or blackberrying up by the chapel near Treveal like I used to. The sun always seemed to be shining then. After it happened I used to go up to the surface often and move amongst the people in the village. I went to see my family, but if I spoke to them they never seemed to hear me and of course they can't see you. You can see them, but they can't see you. That's the worst of it. So I don't go up much now, just to collect wood for the fire and a bit of food now and then. I stay down here with father in the mine and we work away day after day, and from time to time someone like you comes up the tunnel from the sea and lightens our darkness. I shall be sad when you go.'

The old man was hunched over the fire rubbing his hands and holding them out over the heat.

'Not often we have a fire,' he said, his voice more sprightly now. 'Only on special occasions. Birthdays of course, we always have a fire on birthdays back at the cottage. Martha's next. You don't know her; she's my only daughter – she'll be eight on September 10th. She's been poorly you know – her lungs, that's what the doctor said.' He sighed deeply. ''Tis dreadful damp in the cottage. 'Tis well nigh impossible to keep it out.' There was a tremor in the old man's voice that betrayed his emotion. He looked up at Cherry and she could see the tears in his eyes. 'She looks a bit like you, my dear, raven haired and as pretty as a picture; but not so tall, not so tall. Come in closer my dear, you'll be warmer that way.'

Cherry sat with them by the fire till it died away to nothing. She longed to go, to get home amongst the living, but the old man talked on of his family and their little one-room cottage with a ladder to the bedroom where they all huddled together for warmth, of his friends that used to meet in the Tinners' Arms every evening. There were tales of wrecking and smuggling, and all the while the young man sat silent until there was a lull in the story.

'Father,' he said. 'I think our little friend would like to go home now. Shall I take her up as I usually do?' The old man nodded and waved his hand in dismissal.

'Come back and see us sometime, if you've a mind to,' he said, and then put his face in his hands.

'Goodbye,' said Cherry. 'Thank you for the fire and for helping me. I won't forget you.' But the old man never replied.

The journey through the mine was long and difficult. She held fast to the young tinner's waist as they walked silently through the dark tunnels, stopping every now and then to climb a ladder to the lode above until finally they could look up the shaft above them and see the daylight shining in the sky.

'It's dawn,' said the young man, looking up.

'I'll be back in time for breakfast,' said Cherry, setting her foot on the ladder.

'You'll remember me?' the young tinner asked, and Cherry nodded, unable to speak. She felt a strange affinity with him and his father. 'And if you should ever need me, come back again. You may need me and I shall be here. I go nowhere else.'

'Thank you,' said Cherry. 'I won't forget. I doubt anyone is going to believe me when I tell them about you. No one believes in ghosts, not up there.'

'I doubt it too. Be happy, little friend,' he said. And

he was gone, back into the tunnel. Cherry waited until the light from the candle in his hat had vanished and then turned eagerly to the ladder and began to climb up towards the light.

She found herself in a place she knew well, high on the moor by Zennor Quoit. She stood by the ruined mine workings and looked down at the sleeping village shrouded in mist, and the calm blue sea beyond. The storm had passed and there was scarcely a breath of wind even on the moor. It was only ten minutes' walk down through the bracken, across the road by the Eagle's Nest and down the farm track to the cottage where her family would be waiting. She began to run, but the clothes were still heavy and wet and she was soon reduced to a fast walk. All the while she was determining where she would begin her story, wondering how much they would believe. At the top of the lane she stopped to consider how best to make her entrance. Should she ring the bell and be found standing there, or should she just walk in and surprise them there at breakfast? She longed to see the joy on their faces, to feel the warmth of their arms around her and to bask once again in their affection.

She saw as she came round the corner by the cottage that there was a long blue Landrover parked in the lane bristling with aerials. 'Coastguard' she read on the side. As she came down the steps she noticed that the back door of the cottage was open and she could hear voices inside. She stole in on tiptoe. The kitchen was full of uniformed men drinking tea and around the table sat her family, dejection and despair etched on every face. They hadn't seen her yet. One of the uniformed men had put down his cup and was speaking. His voice was low and hushed.

'You're sure the towel is hers, no doubts about it?'

Cherry's mother shook her head.

'It's her towel,' she said quietly, 'and they are her shells. She must have put them up there, must have been the last thing she did.'

Cherry saw her shells spread out on the open towel and stifled a shout of joy.

'We have to say,' he went on, 'we have to say then, most regrettably, that the chances of finding your daughter alive now are very slim. It seems she must have tried to climb the cliff to escape the heavy seas and fallen in. We've scoured the cliff top for miles in both directions and covered the entire beach, and there's no sign of her. She must have been washed out to sea. We must conclude that she is missing, and we have to presume that she is drowned.'

Cherry could listen no longer but burst into the room shouting.

'I'm home, I'm home. Look at me, I'm not drowned at all. I'm here! I'm home!'

The tears were running down her face.

But no one in the room even turned to look in her direction. Her brothers lay on their arms and cried openly, one of them clutching the giant's necklace.

'But it's me,' she shouted again. 'Me, can't you see? It's me and I've come back. I'm all right. Look at me.'

But no one did, and no one heard.

The giant's necklace lay spread out on the table.

'So she'll never finish it after all,' said her mother softly. 'Poor Cherry. Poor dear Cherry.'

And in that one moment Cherry knew and understood that she was right, that she would never finish her necklace, that she belonged no longer with the living but had passed on beyond.

The Horn

SUSAN PRICE

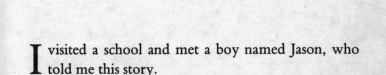

I visited a school and met a boy named Jason, who told me this story.

He said he took some friends from the town to visit a cousin of his who lived in the country. He thought they were going to have a great day, but one of his friends spoilt things by bringing along an older boy named Millfield, who was a real big-head, a right show-off. All the time they were on the bus he kept on about the fights he'd been in, and how much beer he could drink, and all these lies. He had a swastika tattooed on his forehead. He was a proper berk, Jason said.

Jason's cousin Sarah was waiting for them at the bus-stop. She wasn't pleased about Millfield being with them; he was the kind of person who made himself disliked in two minutes. But she didn't say anything because she thought he was one of Jason's friends.

Jason and Sarah took the others round, showing

them the river, and the trees they could climb, and the sandstone cliffs and caves, the woods and all the things they'd come to see. Millfield kept trailing after them saying things like, 'Is this the best there is round here? Ain't you got any pubs, or anything good?' Jason wanted to tell Millfield to clear off, but he didn't, in case Millfield was really as tough as he kept saying he was.

One of the other boys, Adrian, was mad about natural history, and animals, and he got on well with Sarah. When they were in the wood, Sarah started telling him that there'd once been this huge forest there, that had grown right over the Midlands and up into Yorkshire, and this little wood was all there was left of it. But there'd been wolves, and deer, and bears in the forest once, right where they were standing. They were getting proper excited, these two, going on about the wolves and bears, so, of course, Millfield had to come up and start: 'How could a wood go from here to Yorkshire? And there's no bears in England. You're stupid.' And when Sarah said there had been, once, Millfield said, 'Well, so what? Who cares? All these trees are stupid anyway. You should cut 'em all down and build some place you can get a drink.'

Sarah turned her back on him, and asked Adrian if he'd like to see some nestlings; and he said yes, so they went off. The others followed, and Millfield trailed after them, deliberately making a lot of noise, to frighten away any animals that they might see. Jason turned round and saw that Millfield was pulling branches off the trees, breaking saplings in two and just doing damage, for no reason. 'Stop that,' Jason said.

'You going to make me?' Millfield said. Jason had *known* he would say that.

Jason told him that he shouldn't tear the trees, because they were alive. 'They're about as alive as you are,' Millfield said. 'Anyway, if I want to break 'em, I shall, and there's nothing you can do to stop me.' So Jason ignored him, since arguing was only making him worse.

The part of the wood Sarah took them to was quite a way. Every few yards there would be a great rush of birds into the air, and bird-cries all about them, and then a deep silence stretching away through the trees, a silence that seemed to echo with the sound of wings. Sarah said the birds were wood-pigeons, and their being disturbed like that meant that no other people had been there for a long while, and by flying up the birds had warned all the animals in the wood to keep quiet and still.

'The old days must have been like this,' Adrian said. 'Isn't it great?' There was nothing to tell them that it was the twentieth century except their own clothes, and it was so quiet. It could have been Roman times, when there were bears, or the Middle Ages, when there were wolves – they might have gone back in time without noticing it. It was a bit frightening, but really great, Jason said. They thought that, any minute, a bear might come along through the trees – but instead, Millfield came clumping along, saying how stupid everything was. He'd have frightened off any bears that might be about. 'You're the stupid thing,' Jason said to him, and Millfield said, 'I'll put one on you in a minute. You want to take me on? I'll kill you.' He always got you into conversations like that. He was so boring.

'Oh, *shut up*,' Sarah said, and he did. Sarah brought them to where the nestlings were, and they took it in turns to peer into the nest from a distance at the ugly little things, all opening their beaks. They were careful not to get too close, or touch, because Adrian said the parent birds wouldn't come back and feed the little birds if they did; and Sarah said that was right. Then somebody spotted a squirrel, and they turned to watch that. When they looked at the nest again, Millfield was standing there. And he'd taken the nestlings from the nest, and broken their necks, and dropped them on the ground. He stood grinning at them, sort of proud and ashamed at the same time.

They stood and stared at him. Now why had he done a thing like that? What good had it done him? He made you feel sick and tired, Jason said.

Sarah said, 'You'll be sorry you did that.'

'Who's going to make me sorry?' he said. 'You going to get your Dad on to me? I'll kill him. I've got a knife, you know.' And he pulled this knife out of his pocket. He thought he was so tough.

'Let's go,' Sarah said, and walked away, and the others went with her. Millfield followed, shouting that they were scared, scared, scared, and big babies.

They didn't answer him back, because the sound of his shouts among the trees was frightening – not because they were scared of *him* so much, but because it was as if no one should shout like that there – like you shouldn't shout in a church and you feel bad if you do. Millfield's big, yobbish yells echoed from the trees, and travelled a long way, and you got this creepy feeling that *something* – something a long way off – might hear and come. But Millfield went on yelling, because he thought he was annoying them.

The way Sarah was taking them went deeper into the wood, and the paths were more overgrown. It was hard to get through, a lot of the time. Millfield was making a smashing, crashing row, breaking his way through the branches. They came to a little stream, where the ground was black mud. A big tree was growing there, and hanging on the tree was a bow and arrows, and a horn, a real, old-fashioned horn, for blowing, like you see in films. The arrows were in a long bag, made of leather – they could tell by the smell that it was leather – and the arrows smelt of wood and feathers. The bow was hanging by its wooden part from the bag of arrows, and it was a long bow, longer than any of them were tall – except for Millfield, maybe.

They stopped and looked at these things. The stream made a tiny, trickling sound as it ran beside them, but it was dead quiet there. They were scared to speak, or even to make a noise by moving. And they were scared to touch the things, they were so strange. Not the sort of things you expect to find, even in a forest, these days. Who had put them there?

Then Millfield came up and said, 'Somebody's been playing Robin Hood!' And he started shouting, 'Come out, come out, wherever you are! Come out and let's see you in your little tights and your little green hat!' His voice went off for miles through the trees, and kept coming back in echoes. The others heard little, quick rustles of movement in the leaves around them, and then the quiet would be even quieter, until Millfield started bellowing again. If there was somebody about – somebody who'd left that bow and arrows there – then that person could hear Millfield all right, and knew exactly where Millfield and the people with him were – but *they* couldn't hear or see the owner of the bow and arrows.

They told Millfield to be quiet, but that only made him worse. 'Tell you what,' he said, and he was un-hooking the horn from the tree. 'Robin Hood's supposed to come if you blow his horn, isn't he? Shall I blow it and see if he does?'

'Robin Hood blows his horn to call his men,' Sarah said. 'And you'd better leave it alone. You don't know who it belongs to. Put it back.'

'I don't care who it belongs to,' Millfield said, and he blew the horn. It made a peculiar noise, a bit like a trumpet does when it's blown by someone who doesn't know how to play it properly. But he blew it again, two or three times.

Sarah suddenly started running away from the tree,

and they all ran with her – except Millfield. They didn't know why. But as soon as Sarah moved, it was as if she pulled them with her on a string.

You know that feeling you get when you're on your own in the house and you're *positive* that there's somebody standing right behind you, watching you, Jason said. It felt like that after the horn was blown, but it was even more scary, because it was in a forest, not a house. It was as if every tree was alive, just as he'd told Millfield, but alive and staring too. The silence in the forest – which was full of little noises and breaths – got quieter and quieter, but even more full of little noises and movements that you couldn't quite hear or place, but which were all around, on every side. It was as if a net had been put round that place in the forest and was being pulled tighter and tighter, as something came nearer and nearer.

Behind them, they could hear Millfield laughing and calling them names, and tooting on the horn, just as if he hadn't noticed anything – but then they heard him give a yell. They didn't see what had happened to him, because they were facing the other way and running. But Millfield started running himself. They knew, because of the noise he made. And he was yelling at the top of his voice. He sounded really scared, but they couldn't tell what he was saying.

They were out of breath, and they stopped running and listened. All they could hear for a while was Millfield – but then there was another sound. They all recognized what the sound was, but it was a long time before they would admit it, because it was so frightening. A long time after Jason and Sarah told each other what they had thought at the time, and they both agreed that the sound had been the sound that an arrow makes in films and on television. The sound of an arrow being shot from a bow, flying fast through the air, and then hitting something. But since neither of them had ever heard an arrow being shot except on television, they couldn't be sure that was what it was. But after that sound, they didn't hear anything of Millfield.

They were afraid to go looking for him. They all ran home to Sarah's house, and they told Sarah's Mum that they'd lost a friend they'd had with them – they didn't say anything about the horn, or the bow and arrows, or what they'd heard. They were too scared.

Millfield hadn't turned up by the time the boys went home, and he didn't show up at his own home either. So he was reported missing, and people started looking for him. He was found, in the wood, close by where he'd killed the nestlings. He was lying face down in the leaf-mould, with his arms spread out, and he was dead. There was nothing to show why he'd died, and there certainly wasn't an arrow in him. Jason read the report in the newspaper, and listened to it on the television and radio, and none of them said anything about horns, or bows and arrows, or even of there having been anybody near Millfield when he'd died. 'Local boy found dead in wood' – that was all.

There had to be an inquest, and the Coroner said he'd died of heart failure. But he'd only been seventeen. 'So it was weird, wasn't it?' Jason said.

I asked Jason if everything he'd told me was true. He said it was, and he knew it was, because he'd been there.

'It's a good story,' I said. 'Your cousin Sarah was right – there was a forest, hundreds of years ago, that went from the Midlands up into Yorkshire. Know what it was called?'

'Yeah,' Jason said. 'Sarah told me. It was Sherwood Forest. So like I say, it's weird, isn't it?'

Hi! It's Me

MARJORIE DARKE

Understand first that I like to be noticed. Right? Having got that out of the way, I'll explain that I don't mean all heads turning as I walk down the street, like they do if you happen to be a movie star or Barry Sheene or someone. I'm talking about ordinary give and take. A friendly wave of the hand. 'Hi!' shouted as you pass a mate. Things of that sort.

Now don't get me wrong. I don't go round carrying a chip on my shoulder. Normally I don't think about being noticed at all. Why should I? There are plenty of good mates in my life. We chat and fool around and generally have a great time. To tell the truth, I've never given the subject two seconds thought before. But today has changed all that.

I'll explain.

Between leaving the hospital gates and passing Crenshaws, which can't be more than a hundred metres of street, I'd been cut dead three times. Honest! No

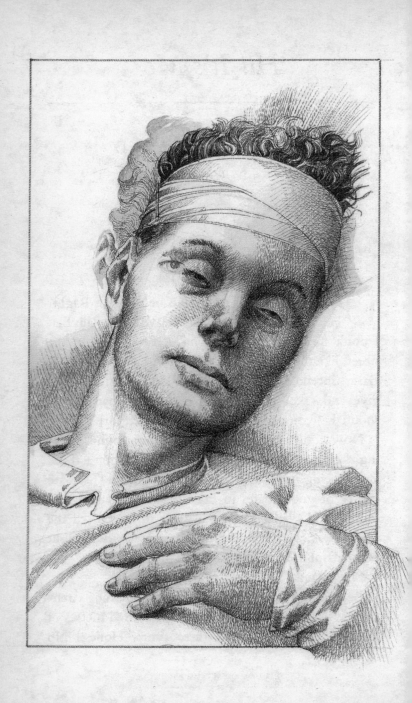

exaggeration. First it was by Bri and Linda. Well . . . they're always gazing at each other so hard it's a wonder they don't walk into lamp-posts or fall down subway steps, so I suppose it was understandable. The second lot I could excuse as well. A bunch of kids from my year at school came yahooing out from the turn-off to the swimming baths. They were all over the place like kangaroos escaped from the zoo. Probably never saw me.

But with Terry it was different.

He came loping along, his great mitts stuffed into his pockets and that spray of dark hair which never will lie flat, standing erect like a yard brush. I could hear him whistling out of tune as usual, and when he came nearer I saw he was looking directly at me.

I met his gaze. 'Hi, Terry!'

He didn't seem to hear. I got the uneasy feeling that something was badly wrong. We were closing in and his eyes, still meeting mine, were totally blank.

I said 'Hi!' again, this time nudging him with my elbow as we drew level, sending him slightly off course. He brushed past as if I was a stranger. Not a flicker of recognition. Not even the faint look of irritation you might throw at someone who had bumped into you accidentally-on-purpose.

'Terry!' I said. Loud.

He went on walking.

'Terry . . . Gerry!' We'd always had this joke about our rhyming names. 'It's me, you berk.'

We were separated now and I watched his skinny

back and long legs moving away down the street. It
was the most skilled freeze-off I'd ever seen. And he
was supposed to be my best mate! I racked my brains
to search out what I'd done to offend him. I couldn't
recall a thing, and anyway, cutting people dead isn't
his style. He can be moody as hell all right, but whatever the cause he's far more likely to react by booting
a Coke can from here to next Tuesday or bellowing
at you in a fog-horn voice than by stalking past like
this.

But there had to be *some* answer. Perhaps if I was to
work my way through yesterday step by step I'd get a
clue. It had been a pretty odd sort of day now I came
to think about it . . . if I could think about it . . .

An unsteady feeling took hold. Not dizziness, but
as if bits of my inside had wrenched loose and were
floating about. Ever since leaving the hospital gates,
something had nagged at me. Now I knew what it
was. A haze, a kind of patchy fog, lay over the time
in hospital and a lot of the previous day. Little corners
were left sticking out here and there, but nothing
joined up. A clear picture of a pudding dish loaded
with jam tart and custard – Terry's face very close as
he shovelled the food into his mouth – fell into my
head. So did the strong urge to push his guzzling mug
down into the sticky yellow gunge. Had I done it? Was
that why he'd treated me to the big freeze? The picture
faded leaving only fog. My face and armpits sweated.
Terry was still in sight, and suddenly furious, I left off
worrying about him. He'd offended *me*!

'Up you then!' I shoved two fingers in the air.

He must have heard me shout, but he didn't turn round. Neither did the old bloke or the woman who were passing arm in arm. There was a girl too, wheeling a pram. She shaved by me with only whiskers to spare. The baby, sitting up, was eating its shoe. None of them paid me the slightest attention. I could have been a litter bin or a road sign or something. It was almost like I wasn't there! I know people can be next thing to blind when they are in town shopping. They go into a sort of trance, eyes glazed as they barge along, crushing toes and carelessly stabbing you with umbrellas. But I really had made a terrible din yelling like that. They *must* have heard. And it's human nature to turn and stare at anyone who makes a racket.

The unsteadiness inside began to grow.

Come on, man, get a hold, I said to myself. What I needed was coffee. It would give me a chance to sit down and sort out my mind. Get yesterday into some sort of order, then the rest would come flooding back (it was a bit of bluff really, but I had to do something to shake myself back into feeling normal). I took a swift butchers at the shop window across the pavement. It was packed with TVs and computers and stuff. Two of the tellys were showing different programmes, and in front, reflected in the plate glass, was *me*. Jeans, red sweater, zipper jacket, all in order. On my feet, as usual, were my new Silver Shadow running shoes. I've been wearing them non-stop for a week (except in bed) because they are so comfortable. Now

I'm not into performing in front of mirrors, but I leapt up and down, waving my arms and pulling faces, just to make absolutely sure it was me, so that the daft notion I'd suddenly gone missing gave up and died.

Phew! A doughnut would be a good idea too, along with the coffee – to build up the old blood-sugar. I've heard you can go bananas in the head if you are low on sugar. You see things that aren't there and want to bash everybody in sight and scream. I hadn't got to that state . . . yet. But there was a scream hovering in the background. It wouldn't take much more before it took me over.

A little way down the street, opposite Marks and Sparks, is a café called Sneakers. Terry and I go there sometimes. It's self-service and you can choose small or large coffee, depending on your cash flow, and their doughnuts are out of this world. Not wanting to spend more energy and shrink my blood-sugar even further by trekking to the zebra crossing, I decided to cut straight across the street. The traffic was thickish, but there was no danger. I had a clear view either way and an island stood in the middle. Besides, I reckon I'm a good judge of distances. A smart grey Rover 2000 purred by, leaving masses of room between its boot and the lorry behind. I'm a good judge of oncoming-vehicle-travelling-speed too. I could get to that island, no problem. So I *thought*. It would have been true as well, if the driver had kept a steady pace, but just as I got out into the road, the brainless idiot stamped on the gas. I'm not making it up. I couldn't believe it either! Twenty tons of metal and giant rubber tyres hurtling straight at me! There was no time to dither or jump back. He wasn't going to stop. It was run or be pancaked.

I ran.

The island seemed like ten kilometres off, but I made it, and managed the other half of the road as well. Afterwards I had to lean against a lamp-post because my legs threatened to give way. The shakes had such a grip I hadn't the nous to bawl at the bonehead driver until he was well down the street – when it was too late.

Town was filling up. A dozen people at least must have passed before I woke up to the fact that not one of them had thrown half a glance my way, or had yelled at the driver, or at me, or had even bothered to ask if I was OK. In some ways that was a relief. If there's one thing I can't stand it's people fussing over you when you don't feel a hundred per cent fit. I waited till the trembling calmed down, then began to weave along the crowded pavement, but it was weird. I felt as though I was on my own.

Sneakers was three-quarters full. Four people were queueing by the counter. I joined them, taking a tray and a plate; helping myself to a doughnut from behind one of the little lift-up glass doors on the counter. The queue shuffled forward. Two small coffees steamed gently near an urn.

'Large coffee, please,' I said to the woman slopping the last dregs of milk from a jug into teacups.

She didn't seem to hear.

I raised my voice a bit. *'Large coffee.'*

She turned away and started fiddling with the Dairy Fresh Milk container, drawing off milk from the tap into her jug.

Being ignored so completely was beginning to get on my wick. I lost my cool. 'What's the matter . . . are you deaf or something?'

Apparently she was, because all that happened was she came back to the cups and went on pouring milk. The last customer before me was paying at the cash desk. He didn't look round. Nobody looked round.

One last try, I thought. *'Coffee. Large.'*

Not a dicky-bird: I could have been shouting from inside a coal-mine for all the effect it was having.

That coffee was a real need now. The woman stopped what she was doing in order to chat to another waitress, turning away from the counter, so I helped myself to a small cup, spilling some because my hands weren't too steady. Sliding the tray along the shelf, I steered it towards the cash desk. The cashier stared at my doughnut, at my cup and saucer . . . and said nothing.

This was getting to be more than a joke. I nipped the back of my hand between finger-nails. The sharp pinch of pain was a real pleasure. Phew! For a minute I thought I'd turned into the Invisible Man! But I was as solid as that cash register. I mean, I really was *there*.

'It adds up to fifty-six pence,' I dumped the money in front of her.

She looked up from my tray to my face. Her large brown eyes had the same glazed-over appearance as shoppers' do. Next to the cash desk was the cutlery tray. My fingers itched to grab a handful of knives and forks and hurl them on the floor. Nobody could ignore that sort of shattering row!

But I didn't. I hate scenes. Anyway I wanted my doughnut and coffee. So I left the coins on the counter and took my tray to a window seat and sat looking out at the people going by. Which is how I came to see Des Martin dashing along. He's our PE teacher and he never walks anywhere like a normal human being. Seeing him brought a bit of yesterday walloping back. Me, head down, bending forwards, arms up, hands grasping the wallbars in the gym ready to pull my legs into the upside-down hanging position. I'd done the exercise heaps of times. It's one of Des Martin's favourite tortures. Only I don't find it that hard and don't get in a sweat like some kids. But yesterday my hands must have been greasy because along with the picture of myself heaving my feet off the floor, was an awful sensation of insecurity. An instant knowing that I wasn't going to be able to hang on. My hands were slipping . . . slipping . . .

Then nothing.

I came back into the café. I was sweating. Gingerly I touched the top of my head. There ought to have been a duck egg-sized lump, or at least a tender bruise. But under my hair (which is pretty thick, so I suppose it must have been some protection) my scalp was unhurt. The hospital doctors had done a good job. I knew about being there. Hadn't I just walked out? And I had an extra memory of waking up in this high bed in a dimly-lit ward with a lot of other patients. Being night time I couldn't see them very well. I was rather woozy anyway. A nurse had come along and given me something to drink. Then I'd gone back to sleep again. Or that's how I think it was.

I'd had enough of being indoors, so I licked the last of the doughnut sugar off my fingers and left the café. The food had done me good, and the sun, which had decided to come out, helped raise my spirits too. Things definitely seemed more cheery outside. Ordinary things were happening. Ordinary people walking about. Ordinary traffic. Ordinary birds flapped overhead.

At the end of the street I could see the entrance to the park. It's only a small, very ordinary park – but that was in its favour right now. There are swings, a slide, a climbing-frame and a puddle they call a pond with a couple of ducks. As I hadn't got much else planned for the present, it seemed a good place to be. I'd just begun walking in that direction, when this little kid in a blue track suit and training shoes very like my Silver Shadows came sprinting past. He was going like the clappers, but his sporty gear didn't fit with the way he moved. His body didn't seem properly laced together. No rhythm in his running; just these arms and legs doing their own thing without bothering about each other. One of his shoelaces had come undone and he stood on it with his other foot, then staggered and would have fallen if he hadn't come up against the park fence. He stood there blinking and catching his breath. I got a proper butchers at his face. Short spiky hair, big ears, a lot of freckles that ran together over cheeks and squashy nose. His top teeth stuck out a bit too. A perky face you would remember, and I got the vague feeling I did. Only I couldn't pin down where I'd seen him before. As I was trying to rack my brains and dig it out, his small, very blue eyes homed in and his gaze latched on to me. It didn't half give me a kick to know I was being watched. Wasn't imagination either because I moved as a test and saw his eyes follow me.

I said: 'Hi! Like your shoes,' and stuck out my foot so he'd see mine were similar.

A big grin spread across his face, which somehow made him less familiar.

'Going to the park?' I asked.

He nodded.

That gave me an even bigger kick. He'd actually heard what I'd said. 'I am too. You'd better do your shoe up before you fall flat.'

He bent down and tied some sort of a knot, then rushed off through the gate as if his mum or somebody was pelting after him, about to drag him away before he could make it to the swings. I followed to see what he would do. A few other kids were larking about in the playground. They didn't take any notice of either of us. He grabbed a swing and scrambled up, standing and trying to get it to go without the slightest idea of how to bend and straighten his knees, leaning forwards then back at the same time. He was useless.

He saw me and shouted: 'Give us a push!'

'Sit down then.'

He slid on to the wooden seat, fidgeting his legs.

'Hang on!' I pushed and he swung away.

'Harder . . . harder . . .' he called.

So I gave him a really good shove the second time, saw him grin and heard his squeal of pleasure as the swing zoomed high in the air. It came back, then swooshed past me, then up again. Everything would have been fine if he'd hung on, but for some reason the little idiot decided he wanted to get off in a hurry and instead of waiting till the swing slowed, he just launched himself at the ground. The chains of the swing rattled and twisted, and the seat caught him a real thwack on the bum which sent him sprawling. It was lucky it was such a low slung swing or it might have clouted his head.

'You OK?' For a minute I was worried.

'Yes.' He rolled over and sat up. Dust and muck covered the front of his track suit and his hands were filthy, but there wasn't a scratch on him.

'You daft twit! What did y'do a stupid thing like that for?' I was a bit angry because he'd scared me.

'I want to go on the slide.'

'You could've waited till the swing stopped.'

He didn't bother to answer, but scrambled up and dashed to the slide, tripping twice as he climbed the steps, then choosing to come down head first, falling off at the bottom. This didn't hold him back. He just got up and did the same thing all over again. He was a nut-case. I might have left him to kill himself on his own, only by now I felt sort of attached to him as he'd been the only one to take any notice of me this morning. Being connected made me feel kind of responsible too. No one else seemed to be keeping an eye on him and he couldn't have been much more than seven at the outside.

'Let's have a look at the ducks,' I suggested.

It was a waste of breath. He was already half-way up the slide steps again. When he reached the bottom a third time and shot off the end, there was a dog nosing under the slide. They collided. I'm sure they did, but the funny thing was the dog hardly shifted. It did have four stocky legs well spread out, one at each corner, but the kid had been travelling at quite a speed. I watched as he got to his feet. There was dirt on his face as well now. I expected him to make a bee-line back up the steps, but he didn't. He put a hand out and scratched between the dog's pointed ears.

'Hello, dog.'

Well . . . you'd have thought he'd let off a firework between its back legs or something. That animal leapt about ten feet in the air. The hairs of its rough black coat bristled and it growled, backing away to a safe distance, where it stopped and began to bark like a maniac. On and on.

Now dogs generally aren't my scene. I'm not scared

of them. They just bore me. If I'd been on my own I'd have probably pushed off and left the thing to have its nervous breakdown, but the little kid was different. I reckon he had a death wish – and like I said, I felt sort of responsible. So I hung about and watched him walk over, holding out his mucky hand and calling: 'Dog, dog . . . come here dog . . .' The nearer he got the more frantic that half-baked animal became. I got quite hooked watching the pair of them. The kid moving – forwards. The dog moving – backwards. Both at the same pace. A crazy sort of dance. How much longer they'd have gone on this way I don't know, but there was an interruption. A shout,

'Violet. Come here . . . Violet!'

I looked to see which was Violet. None of the kids in the playground budged. They didn't even turn round. The bloke who had shouted came walking briskly across the grass towards us. He had one of those droopy moustaches hung on to a red face. In fact he looked half boiled in his thick padded jacket – not surprising now the sun was beaming down.

'Violet!' he reached the dog and took hold of its collar.

Only then did I see he was carrying a leash. Violet! I creased up. I couldn't help it. The little kid didn't seem to twig the funny side and just stood staring. Violet didn't let up; whining and pulling away.

'What's the matter, girl?' The bloke fastened the leash. 'Give over will you!' He dragged the animal towards the path, almost barging into the little kid who happened to be standing in the way. The kid took a step back. Of course he was standing on his shoelace again. And of course he went splat! Violet growled and leapt over him. The bloke couldn't have cared less. He didn't look back – just barged on towards the gate.

That really bugged me. Who did he think he was, crashing about and shoving people out of the way as if he owned the whole park?

I shouted, 'What happened to your contact lenses, mate? Why don't you look where you're going?' I was really steaming.

He didn't trouble to glance over his shoulder even then. But the little kid gave me a startled look as he got to his feet. I thought maybe I'd scared him. I didn't want him to run off.

'What's your name?' I asked quickly.

'Peter. What's yours?'

'Gerry. D'you live round here?'

'Yes.' He looked faintly worried.

'What's up? Doesn't your mum know you're in the park?'

No answer. He was fishing in his trouser pocket, then in the pocket of his track top. 'It's gone. I've lost it.' He looked round in a helpless sort of way.

'Lost what?'

'Digger,' was all he said and then rushed off. Not sensibly back to the playground, but out of the gate. Just what I hadn't wanted.

'Hey!' I ran after him.

There weren't all that many people this end of the street now, but I couldn't see him anywhere. He'd done a complete disappearing job. For some reason that upset me. We'd only knocked around together for about half an hour, yet I still felt in some way responsible for him, which was nutty. He was nothing to do with me. I went back to the playground because there didn't seem much else to do. One or two people were ambling about, but the place felt curiously empty. I mooched past the swings, going to the slide, not expecting to find anything. After all I didn't even know what I was looking *for*. Then, quite by accident, my foot kicked against something hard. Funny how that sort of thing can happen when you aren't trying at all. Other times you can go round with a gold-plated magnifying glass and not find so much as a pin!

I felt about and pulled out one of those old-fashioned Dinky toys. It was pretty battered, but you could see what it was – a mechanical digger. And the little nut had gone charging off without saying where he lived! I stuffed it in my pocket. Serve him right if I kept it.

The park was suddenly boring. So I left. Just outside the gates was a stone, perfect for dribbling, and I did some real Kevin Keegan stuff along the pavement. It needed fine judgement and a lot of concentration to flip it round the walking feet without bumping into the bodies on top. I was really into it and got quite skilled, passing Sneakers without noticing and drawing level with the telly shop, where I'd seen my reflection, before realizing I was heading straight back to hospital.

That was a jolt.

Oughtn't I to be heading the other way – home?

What time was it?

There was a pale stripe of skin round my wrist where my watch should have been. Grit brains! I must have left it on the hospital locker when I got dressed. I shut my eyes, trying to get a picture of myself dressing, but all I could see was sun colours printed on the insides of my eyelids. That wasn't all though. A sticky question reared up and wouldn't go away. If I'd spent the night in hospital and now was up and dressed, other things were missing besides my watch. Where were my pyjamas and my washing kit? And another thing, how had I come away from hospital without Mum? She'd never let me go home on my own after being kept in overnight. I know she works till one at the factory on Saturdays, but I was positive she'd get time off.

It was Saturday, wasn't it?

I sprinted back across the road without trouble this time, and flattened my nose against the shop window. 'Grandstand' the telly screen said with titles unrolling. Saturday lunchtime. No doubt about it.

Perhaps Mum was already at the hospital? If she found I was missing she'd be doing her nut. She doesn't mind about making scenes. If she thinks it's necessary, you find you're into a show that's better than Dallas before you can say JR! I could picture it all. Mum creating like mad. Receptionists running round in circles. Nurses and doctors pinned to the wall by their ears.

I belted through the hospital gates, through Outpatients, through swing doors into a blue and cream corridor. My Silver Shadows padded softly over the plastic floor tiles with hardly a sound. I switched into automatic pilot at the staircase, going up two at a time, not really knowing where I was heading only that it seemed right.

But maybe it would be as well to check up?

I spotted two nurses coming towards me. 'Excuse me?'

They went past. Chatting.

A porter came from behind. As he reached me I said, 'Excuse me?'

He swerved right, steering the empty trolley he was pushing into an open lift. The gates rattled shut.

The hospital was overheated like they always are, but it felt as if someone had poured icy water down my back. I shuddered.

They were treating me like I was a ghost!

Not even that. Nobody was scared except me.

Taking a deep breath, I pushed on.

Kitchen, bathroom, toilets, several closed doors, and the corridor ended in a sort of mini foyer with doorways leading off either side; the main ward in front. Back to base! I'd have known even if I hadn't heard the murmur of Mum's voice coming from behind a half open door labelled Ward Sister. She wasn't shouting, surprise surprise! I had half a mind to stroll in and join her, but something happened that drove everything else out of my head.

From where I was standing I had an angled view of a bed. The usual high hospital sort with metal ends and a prop for supporting pillows and whoever happens to be in it. Hospital beds, with or without patients, are always tidy with bedclothes tucked tight under the mattress. But this bed was different. A tornado seemed to have hit it. Pillows, sheets, blankets made a rickety hill in the middle. The green coverlet was dragged half over the side, half lying on the floor. Scrabbling in amongst the chaos was a kid in stripy pyjamas. He emerged for an instant and I had this clear view of spiky hair and freckles like syrup spreading over squashed-up nose and cheeks. Then he was gone again like a mole tunnelling in earth.

You could have knocked me down with a bus ticket. Still in a daze I put my hand in my pocket. The mechanical digger was *there*. Collecting my scattered wits, I started off towards the exploded bed, but before I'd taken more than a few paces, a nurse came bellowing up to Peter (yes, *Peter* . . . my mind was boggling) and started giving him a real telling off. She whisked him up and plonked him in a chair, then began sorting out the bedclothes. Her broad, energetic back kept moving between us, so I couldn't be sure if he'd noticed me. I didn't doubt it was the digger that he was hunting for, but it wasn't the right moment to charge across and hand him the cause of the trouble. I decided to hang on. The nurse certainly hadn't finished all she wanted to say. I caught a word here and there.

'. . . concussion . . . supposed to keep quiet . . . romping about . . . have to lie down . . .'

The word 'concussion' fixed in my brain. So he'd bashed his head too. I wasn't surprised.

In the ward were eight beds. Six (not counting Peter's) had patients in them – all glued to the bed-making drama. The remaining bed, across the central aisle from Peter's and close to me now, was hidden by green flowery curtains.

I never had found out the rules about visiting times, but a quick glance told me no visitors were here. That bossy nurse had almost finished remaking the bed. I didn't want her ordering me out before I'd had time to discover what was going on. Taking a chance on my being ignored by her was too great a risk, even though nearly everyone else had been acting as if I didn't exist.

She gave a final smooth to the coverlet. On impulse I took the only hiding place to hand, sliding between the flowery curtains. I meant to say a reassuring word to whoever was in the hidden bed. No point in rousing complaints that might bring the nurse running. So I turned round to face the bed.

He lay quite still, eyes closed, a bandage round his forehead and a plaster across the bridge of his nose. One closed eyelid was swollen and purpling. A cold trickle of disbelief started somewhere behind my ears and went on travelling. A quarter of me felt it while the other three-quarters gaped down at *myself*.

So I *was* a ghost!

Then my body went numb as well. Thinking was out of the question. After what seemed like a thousand years a very slow message passed back from my eyes to my paralysed brain.

The body in the bed – *my body* – was breathing.

Relief made the floor sway and it was a case of sitting on the bed or falling. I sat, staring at the coverlet moving gently up and down, up and down. It was a pretty good sight. I still couldn't reason, but a tiny stir of curiosity made me shift up the bed to get a better look at myself. Something wasn't quite right, and I don't mean the plaster or bandage or the black eye. I put out a nervous finger and prodded the nose-plaster. Not hard – very gently. A stab of pain crossed my face. Quickly I brought my hand back to feel my nose. No plaster, but the pain had been real. It set my brain-wheels turning and I began to twig what was wrong. That *was* me in the bed – the pain was proof. Up until now I'd only ever seen myself as a back-to-front mirror image. This was the first time I'd ever seen myself as other people see me.

From beyond the curtains came the squeak of shoes. A voice said:

'You can sit with him a while if you like, Mrs Baines. He's sleeping now.'

And Mum's voice. 'I'll stay till he wakes. My husband's home so I've plenty of time.'

I thought – she'll have hysterics when she sees two of me . . . *if* she does. I couldn't stand either possibility.

No time for making plans. I did the only thing I
could think of on the spur of the moment. Lifting up
the covers, I got into bed with myself and shut my
eyes. There wasn't even time to take off my Silver
Shadows.

The curtains were drawn back.

'Gerry?' Mum said.

I opened one eye wide. The other remained a slit.
My body felt as if I'd done ten rounds with Muham-
med Ali or somebody. Under the bandage my forehead was sore. I did manage a creaky sort of smile.

'How are you?'

'Battered.' I felt about under the sheet, half
expecting to find two of me still in the bed.

'Uncomfortable, are you? Here, let me straighten
your pillows.'

'Don't fuss, Mum. I'm OK.' But I wasn't. Not
really. My head ached and my one eye felt as tight as
a blown-up balloon. All the same I did seem to have
got together with myself.

The foot of the bed was no longer screened by
curtains and the little kid, Peter, was standing in the
middle of the aisle, staring. He grinned at me. I knew
now why that grin had been unfamiliar in the park.
The only other time I'd seen him before was here, and
he'd been asleep. He came and stood at the bottom of
my bed.

'Mum,' I said, 'feel in the pocket of my jeans.'

She smiled and shook her head. 'I took those home
last night while you were still out for the count.'

From nowhere she produced my dressing-gown and drew the digger from the pocket like a conjuring trick. 'This what you were after?'

'It belongs to him.' I gave up trying to fathom what was going on. I'd been out of my head, that's for sure. Out of my body too, unless I'd gone round the bend.

Peter was grinning from ear to ear. He took the digger. 'Where did you find it?'

'Oh . . . somewhere. On the floor.' It was the best I could do.

Mum stayed on a bit. We had tea, and after, she went home. Later Terry came to visit me.

'Hi! You look terrible,' he said. 'Have a Liquorice Allsort.'

'Thanks,' I took a soft coconut. 'You look beautiful.'

He loomed over me, grinning and shaking his fist. 'Want a punch in your other eye?'

'Get lost!'

'You want to watch it, matey!' He sat down by the bed and helped himself from the box of sweets again, then held them out. 'Have another?'

But eating was too difficult, so Terry munched them for me while he gave a run-down on the snooker I'd missed that afternoon on telly. Then he described the horror film I'd missed out on last night. He talked a lot. Once he gets going, Terry can chew your ear off. Eventually he stopped and chomped several more Liquorice Allsorts.

To fill up the silence I asked, 'Where were you off to whistling down High Street this morning?' As soon as the words were out I realized I'd dropped myself in it.

'Coming here of course. To see how much uglier you'd made your ugly mug. They wouldn't let me in the ward though . . .' he stopped suddenly, staring at me. There was a long pause while he went on staring. Then he said slowly: 'How did you know?'

How *did* I know? Perhaps I was going off my rocker? My head felt clogged, brains fizzing as I tried to think of a good answer. I finally dragged out,

'Somebody told me.'

Terry seemed to believe this. Stuffing the last Liquorice Allsort into his mouth he began rabbiting on about the telly programmes I was going to miss this evening.

I relaxed back on the pillows. I couldn't care less about the telly. It was just so good being back in my own skin.

A Ghost of One's Own

Ursula Moray Williams

Harriet was in the bus, on her way to a party, carrying her family ghost in a basket. She was going to see Miss Meadie, who was giving the party at her home. Her brother William sat on the seat opposite to her, looking sulky, because he had not wanted to come.

Some people can see ghosts and some cannot. Harriet, alone of all her family, could. Her brother William could not, but he could feel them and hear them. And he could smell them, for some ghosts have a fragrance very like old herbs and roses. William did not care for ghosts, so this caused him a lot of inconvenience.

The rest of the family just did not believe in them at all. So they would not be likely to take any notice of the advertisement in a column of the local paper that said: 'All Ghosts Welcome at Miss Meadie's Party on Friday Next.' It did not say who Miss Meadie was,

nor where she lived, but anyone who really wanted to go to the party could surely find out.

Harriet had found out long ago, before she had a ghost of her own, when she was riding her bicycle back from school and had turned aside to explore the driveway of an old country estate. Harriet recognized it at once as ghost territory, even before she met Miss Meadie coming down the drive carrying armfuls of freshly-cut phantom roses which could not possibly be real, since it was February. There was a ghost dog at her heels, and a real one, and two semi-invisible cats, also an old butler, who looked at Harriet and vanished.

Miss Meadie recognized Harriet at once as a Ghost Believer. She gave her a rose and invited her to tea.

'You must come and visit me whenever you like!' Miss Meadie told her. 'And bring your friends with you. I mean your personal friends of course, not your flesh-and-blood ones. I know just what it is like to have your dear ones snubbed and slighted and ignored and not believed in. You must bring them to me instead!'

Harriet was too embarrassed to explain that she had no phantom of her own at present. True, she saw and heard other people's wherever she went, but they all belonged to someone else.

'You do have a ghost of your own, I suppose?' Miss Meadie said sharply, and for a moment Harriet felt that she had arrived under false pretences.

She saved herself by saying calmly: 'Well, just at

present I haven't got one, but my brother William has a skeleton.'

'A skeleton?' said Miss Meadie with interest. 'And why has he not come to see me?'

'My brother,' Harriet explained, 'doesn't like ghosts!'

'Doesn't *like* them?' Miss Meadie repeated. 'But they are lovely things! So gentle! So affectionate . . . so beautiful! Why doesn't your brother William think that ghosts are beautiful?'

'My brother can't *see* ghosts,' Harriet explained. 'He can only hear and feel them. It makes it difficult for him. But he found the skeleton in the loft, himself, and although he can't see it he seems very fond of it. It goes everywhere with him, except to school. It is a very quiet skeleton, only sometimes it has some mischievous ways. It trips up my father in the hall when William leaves it around. My father does not believe in ghosts at all.'

'So sad!' said Miss Meadie. 'So sad!'

'I must be going now,' said Harriet.

'Very well,' said Miss Meadie. 'Come back when you have a ghost of your own.'

Harriet felt that she had fallen short of Miss Meadie's expectations. The parting was a little cold. But she had no idea where she could get a ghost for herself. You couldn't buy them, and William's had arrived quite by accident, due to rummaging in the loft on a wet day in the holidays. As far as Harriet was concerned, he was welcome to it. She did not care for skeletons, but since meeting Miss Meadie she had realized that just seeing ghosts was not enough for a true ghost lover. One ought to have a phantom of one's own.

She did, quite soon.

Harriet and William lived in one half of a semi-detached Victorian villa. The baby belonging to the people in the other half cried all night long, but when their mother mentioned it to the baby's mother she was most indignant, and said that the baby slept in her room and never woke up all night, ever.

'I didn't hear it myself. It was the children who mentioned it.' Harriet's mother said, apologizing hastily.

The next time the baby cried, Harriet took a torch, woke her brother William, and climbed the stairs to the loft. There was a thin partition between their part of the loft and the next-door part. The baby was crying on the other side. Harriet made a hole in the partition, clambered through, and found the baby lying in an old-fashioned basket cradle. The moment it saw her, it stopped crying and smiled.

It was a lovely fat ghostling baby. William, shining the torch for Harriet, could not see it at all, but he was forced to admit it was there when Harriet thrust its warm, curly head against his fingers. She carried it downstairs to her room, and cuddled it and loved it and thought of little else for days and days. Sometimes she fed it on bread and milk, but ghost babies do well enough living on air.

Now she had her baby ghost and William had his skeleton. Their mother could not make them out at all.

'My children have almost *too* much imagination!' she complained to her friends. 'They play all day long with imaginary companions! Harriet pretends she is looking after a baby! She pushes it out in an old doll's pram that she hasn't looked at for years. She is really much too big to push a doll's pram. And William carries round a polythene shopping bag as if there was something precious inside it! Perhaps they are geniuses! I don't know!'

So here they were, going to Miss Meadie's party by bus, since it was difficult to take either the baby or the skeleton on a bicycle, and William was a little sulky because he had not wanted to go, but Harriet had persuaded him it would be hard luck on the skeleton if he didn't.

Harriet had been to visit Miss Meadie just once more, after she had found the baby.

'Good!' said Miss Meadie. 'It is just in time to come to my ghost party.'

Harriet stared.

'I give a ghost party every year,' Miss Meadie went on. 'On Hallowe'en, of course! The patrons like it and it keeps the ghosts off the streets. You can come!'

'And William?' asked Harriet.

'If that is the skeleton boy, then of course he can come,' said Miss Meadie. 'But don't tell all and sundry.

I only want people *with* ghosts, not people without, and I don't want newspapermen or the general public. They might win the game and that would be a pity.'

'What game?' asked Harriet at once.

'Why, the Wishing Bean game!' said Miss Meadie. 'The darling ghosties look forward to it all the year round. You see, after everybody has eaten all they can, I bring on a great dish of hot spiced curry, very hot and very spicy, and somewhere in it there is hidden a little round yellow bean. Everybody eats and eats and eats in the hope that the bean will be found in their portion, because if it is . . .'

'What?' asked Harriet, excited.

'They have a wish!' said Miss Meadie. 'And the wish comes true. Always. Just that one wish, at that one moment in the year.'

'What do they usually wish for?' asked Harriet, wondering what a ghost could desire on such an occasion.

'You never can tell!' said Miss Meadie, shaking her head. 'The very strangest things! There was a cavalier – you know, the kind of fellow who carries his head under his arm. We were all so pleased when he got the bean. We felt sure he would wish to have his head put back on his shoulders again. Well, wouldn't you? But not a bit of it! He wished for a really dashing hat with white feathers in it! He said he would be able to admire it much more easily if he wore it underneath his arm.'

'What else did they wish for?' asked Harriet.

'Well, there was a lady who had been drowned,' said Miss Meadie. 'She wished for a modern permanent wave, because they did not have them in her day. But sometimes it isn't the ghosties who get the bean. Sometimes it's the patrons, and some are very selfish. They wish for cruises in the Mediterranean and things like that which their dear ones can't take part in. One of them wanted a flat in Paris. His ghost couldn't go *there* – it couldn't understand French! So selfish, wasn't it?'

'Can they wish for just anything?' asked Harriet.

'Just anything!' said Miss Meadie. 'And when I think of all the wasted opportunities, I sometimes think I'll never give a party again.'

Harriet immediately began to think what she would wish for if she got the bean at Miss Meadie's party, and she decided on a really beautiful perambulator for the baby, that she could push around without being told that she was really too old for a doll's pram.

'I think it is very kind indeed of you to give a party for us and our ghosts,' she told Miss Meadie. 'Everyone must be very grateful to you.'

'Well, we have our enemies, of course,' said Miss Meadie. 'No doubt you read the advertisement in the paper under the heading "Miscellaneous"?'

Harriet had not. Miss Meadie handed her the paper.

'"Let me solve your psychic problems",' Harriet read aloud. 'Is it advertising medicine?'

'*Psychic*, not *physic*!' said Miss Meadie, fondling the two ghost cats that were sparring for her attention. 'Read on!'

'"Exorcizer guarantees to rid you of pests, black-beetles and all unnatural phenomena for a moderate fee. Apply: Rid-a-Ghoster, Telephone 0000007. All correspondence answered."'

'How silly!' said Harriet. 'I bet he can't do it!'

'Don't be too sure,' said Miss Meadie. '*We* love our ghosties, so they are safe with us, but hatred is very dangerous. It destroys. And I don't believe that Mr Rid-a-Ghoster is a true exorcist or he wouldn't do it for money. A real exorcist helps our friends into another world with love and tenderness, if they really want to go. *He* does it with their consent and co-operation. This man is just out to make money.'

'Well, he shan't have *my* little ghost, or William's!' said Harriet firmly.

The bus shook and jolted. William's skeleton got out of the bag and sat beside him on the seat, since there were very few passengers. The baby slept contentedly in Harriet's basket. She kept peeping at it to see if it was awake or not.

'What have you got in there, love?' asked the woman sitting next to her. 'Is it a kitten?'

'No,' said Harriet, going red.

'Is it a bunny, then?'

'No!' said Harriet, furious with herself for having made loving noises to the baby ghost. 'It's nothing at all!' she added firmly.

The lady was too inquisitive to let that pass. She

leaned across Harriet as if to peer inside the basket. The baby woke up and cried.

'Look! It's nothing at all!' Harriet repeated defiantly. She thrust the basket under the lady's nose and saw the look of surprise that came into her face when she realized that, in fact, it appeared perfectly empty. William, who had been dozing, woke up with a jerk.

'Why's it crying?' he asked loudly.

The skeleton kicked him.

'Ouch!' William said, rubbing his shin. 'You didn't have to do that! I wish I hadn't brought you!'

The lady sat back, looking perfectly astonished, and the bus, arriving at a bus stop, ground to a halt. William, still rubbing his shin, was avenged when a new passenger sat down solidly on top of his skeleton, though only Harriet could see its indignant limbs sticking out on either side of the tweed-coated gentleman who had almost obliterated it.

And suddenly she noticed that the newcomer himself was not without his attendant sprites. His pockets were full of small poltergeists, busy unpicking his buttons, unravelling his pipe tobacco and making holes in his handkerchief. The man seemed to be only half aware of them, but Harriet could see that he was a worried person.

Before the bus restarted, a cloppetting of hooves down the road brought Harriet's head round with a jerk. A man was running at full speed to catch the bus, holding by a rope an enormous grey mare with fiery eyes and the sort of transparency about it that

Harriet had long since learned to associate with phantoms. William looked round too, but when the man had leapt on board he took no further notice. He was stroking the skeleton's hand as it clung to his knee for reassurance. Harriet saw that the horse was attempting to board the bus as well.

'Step along please!' the conductor said, as the man stopped to buy his ticket.

The horse reared up and came down with one of its forefeet fair and square on the conductor's toe. Harriet winced, but the conductor went on punching the ticket as if nothing had happened, and then moved away down the bus, while the man tied the horse's rope to the rail inside the door and sat down on the other side of Harriet, breathing heavily. The horse's hooves pounded along behind, breaking into a gallop as the bus gathered speed.

The horse's owner was staring across at William and William's neighbour as if his eyes would pop out of his head. Harriet realized that the man had noticed something, but just how much she could not tell. To test him, she opened the basket, and the baby began to cry. Harriet took it in her arms.

'Cor! Nice little kid!' said the man admiringly, and then, in a tone of relief: 'You going to Miss Meadie's party, then?'

Harriet realized that her neighbour too had the gift of seeing Other Things. She nodded.

'Didn't see you there last year,' the man went on conversationally. 'Is that your brother across the way?

He's like you. That chap beside him, what's sitting on all those bones, he's a funny one, he is. He's stark staring terrified of those little tiddlers playing up and down his weskit. He brings 'em every year hoping Miss Meadie will get rid of 'em for him, but she loves 'em, bless her heart. Now I wouldn't mind a snuff-out powder for my horse! He's a right nuisance, kicking his stall to pieces when the moon is full and when hounds go by – well! You can't hold him! He's after 'em, and every dog of 'em puts its tail between its legs and hares for home! No wonder all the foxes run straight for my place! You can see 'em laughing! But the Hunt thinks I does it on purpose.'

'Bad luck!' said Harriet.

'Anyway, I've had enough,' said the man. 'This year I'm getting rid of him. There's a chap coming to Miss Meadie's party that can settle things for good and all. An exorcist, he's called. I believe he's a dab hand at ghosts.'

Harriet was just opening her mouth to say that Miss Meadie would never invite anyone like that to her party, when the bus stopped again, a new passenger got on, and immediately, in front of Harriet's very eyes, every ghost went out like a light.

The baby, which had been kicking and chuckling, began to cry bitterly, and Harriet rocked it to and fro to comfort it.

Opposite, the skeleton somehow eased itself out from beneath the body of the man on top and folded itself back into William's bag. The little poltergeists became as flat as shadows and disappeared inside various pockets. Their patron, who seemed to have even less awareness than William, remained staring straight ahead of him with his hands on his knees, while the newcomer walked quietly to the very front of the bus and sat down. He wore a wide-brimmed black hat, and a long black coat. His ears stuck out slightly, and he had a long, thin nose.

Harriet was acutely aware of something wrong about him. He looked just horrid: The horse-owner suddenly noticed him too.

'That's the bloke!' he muttered to Harriet. 'That's the Rid-a-Ghost man! He's going to do quite a bit of business at the party, he told me. I'm not the only one wanting to get rid of a ghostie. Just look at my old grey mare there! Her's got the message!'

Outside the bus, in fact, the grey mare, with her ears laid flat back against her head, could be seen straining against the rope that pulled her. Faintly, at William's feet, the skeleton's teeth could be heard chattering inside the carrier bag.

While the horse's owner moved down the bus to speak confidentially to the uncanny stranger, Harriet noticed that the knot securing the horse's rope to the rail was on the point of coming undone.

'Hold the baby a minute!' she said to William, dumping it on his knees.

'It'll wet,' said William gingerly.

'No, it won't, you twit! It will only feel as if it does!' said Harriet, dashing up the bus. She seized the rope just as the horse was about to break away, and tied it securely to the rail.

'Hey!' shouted the conductor. 'Don't get off before the bus stops!' But the bus was already slowing down.

Nearly everybody got off at the stop nearest to Miss Meadie's. Harriet got off first. She flew up the drive to warn Miss Meadie about the unwelcome visitor who was about to invade the party. But Miss Meadie, busy receiving a score of invited guests, had little time to listen to what Harriet was saying.

Patron after patron, ghost after ghost, were being welcomed into the hall and shown to their seats at a long table which was piled with all kinds of delicious food. When everyone was in their places, Harriet saw to her great relief that the Rid-a-Ghoster was not, after all, among them. Perhaps his courage had failed him in the face of such a happy throng of friends and phantoms, now raising their glasses to toast Miss Meadie, and drinking to the Past, the Happy Past and the Past Again.

Watching the enthusiasm of ghosts and patrons alike, Harriet found it hard to believe that any of these loyal guests could be planning to jettison their phantom friends before the evening was out. She clutched the ghostling baby more closely to her, and noticed that William and his skeleton were fondly sharing a dish of trifle, and clinking spoons.

The evening passed with feasting and music, the excitement growing more intense as one phantom after another burst into song, and everybody joined in. The horse neighed after every verse, the skeleton danced a fandango on the table, the poltergeists pelted everyone with popcorn and Miss Meadie called them her naughty little piglets.

Then at last she clapped her hands, and silence fell.

'We have now come to the climax of our feast!' announced Miss Meadie. 'I shall bring in the dish of the Wishing Bean. You all know what to do! Each one will serve himself with as large a portion as he is still able to eat, and in one of the portions will be found a small, round bean! Whoever finds it can wish one wish aloud, and that wish is bound to come true. Blessings on you all, and may the lucky one's dreams be realized!'

There was a burst of applause as she rose to leave the table, followed by the phantom butler and several dogs and cats, some quite transparent and others with the normal complement of heads, tails and whiskers. Harriet watched her go with mounting excitement. The great moment of the day had arrived! And everyone, *everyone*, had a chance to win. Even the baby would have to be woken up to taste its portion.

But when she looked back again at the table, the Rid-a-Ghoster was sitting in Miss Meadie's chair. Where he had come from nobody could say, but he did not give them time to wonder.

'Friends!' he shouted, leaping to his feet. 'The fun and games are over! The phantoms have had their day! Life is not a party for the dead-and-gone before! Life goes on, tomorrow and the next day and the next, and the one after! Do we want to remain in the thraldom of our hauntings? Do we want to hear again the cryings in the dark, the knockings on the door, the trippings-up and the trippings-in? Do we want our cats' fur standing on end? Our dogs crouching in corners with their tails between their legs? Our plates and cups and saucers hurled about our heads? Do we want to be controlled all our lives long by these wretched manifestations we call ghosts, for want of a better name for them? No! No! Many of you have already come to me for help in ridding you of these pests. Many of you have asked me to meet you here tonight in order to destroy these – these black-beetles! Pah! But I am your friend! Trust in the Rid-a-Ghoster and you shall be freed from your fears! Five pounds please, paid in advance!'

Harriet sat horrified. She saw some of the patrons, looking sheepishly at each other. Two or three put their hands into their pockets, searching for money. A few pound notes were already passing into the Rid-a-Ghoster's greedy palm.

The kitchen door was flung open and Miss Meadie appeared, bearing a steaming dish. She gave one look at the Rid-a-Ghoster and banged the dish down on the table in front of him.

'My seat, if you please,' she said curtly.

Unwillingly, the Rid-a-Ghoster gave it up to her. 'I remain at your service!' he announced to the table at large. 'Whoever wishes to avail themselves of my powers may come with me into the next room. Bring your phantoms with you. Those who have already paid will be served first.'

He was about to retire when he saw that the attention of the whole company was riveted on the Wishing Dish. Nobody wanted to lose their chance of finding the wonderful bean. Those who wished to be exorcized decided to have it done afterwards.

Reluctantly the Rid-a-Ghoster sat down among the rest, and before he could be prevented, he snatched an ample portion of the dish's contents as it circled the table.

The bean was too small to be seen with the naked eye, but Miss Meadie assured everyone that they would know it when they found it on their tongues.

An atmosphere of intense expectation filled the room. Everybody wanted to find the precious bean, and one could almost see the shadows of the various wishes flitting round the table.

Harriet was terribly anxious. There were at least forty chances to one against her winning the bean. She did not even expect to get it. Supposing William got it? If he were sitting nearer to her she could tell him what to wish for, but that was not allowed.

Suppose the horse got it? Nobody would even know. It had swallowed its portion already, and the bean might have gone down with it as far as anyone could tell. Suppose one of the poltergeists got it? They were bound to do something silly with it – they were that sort of person. Suppose the baby got it? But, after the first mouthful, it went back to sleep and Harriet ate its share herself.

The company chewed on. The hall was very quiet now, everyone glancing covertly at his neighbour, dreading any hesitation that might signal the finding of the bean.

The worst thing that could happen, Harriet decided, was that the Rid-a-Ghoster should get it. He was quite capable of destroying every phantom in the room if he did. He ate with concentration, carefully chewing every mouthful to the end and sometimes looking up to catch Harriet's eye upon him.

'If he gets it,' Harriet thought, 'I know he will get rid of the baby and I'll never see it again. I couldn't bear it! I'd just die! And Miss Meadie will die, too, if he destroys all the darling ghosts that she loves so much . . .'

Even Miss Meadie was chewing desperately, keeping her eye meanwhile on the Rid-a-Ghost man. She was almost willing him not to find the bean.

All of a sudden, the Rid-a-Ghoster stopped eating, and choked.

The whole table froze, stopped their own chewing, and looked at him. The Rid-a-Ghoster leaned over the table, coughing and spluttering while the skeleton kindly beat him on the back between the shoulder blades.

The Rid-a-Ghoster searched for a handkerchief in his pocket and put it to his lips.

'He's got it!' Harriet said to herself, feeling quite faint. 'He's got it . . . he's got the bean!'

At that moment her own tongue met something

hard inside her mouth. She pushed it impatiently aside and was about to swallow it when the piercing realization of what it might be, of what it actually *was*, arrested her in the middle of her swallow. Quickly she put her hand to her mouth and removed a tiny, hard round bean from the back of her tongue. Even when she saw it lying in the palm of her hand, she could hardly believe it.

'I've got the bean!' Harriet announced.

Her first feeling was of such pure relief that she wanted to burst into tears. The Rid-a-Ghoster, whatever else he might do, could not now destroy them all. Then all the wishes that she had ever wished for came crowding into her head, wishes for her family, wishes for herself, wishes for the people.

But the wish that came bursting from her lips even before she found words to say it went ringing round the table, and everyone stared and listened, and listened and stared again, as Harriet shouted:

'I wish that all the ghosts in this room were real people for ever and ever and ever!'

A hush fell upon Miss Meadie's table, and one by one each guest looked at one another. Nobody said a word, until the horse's owner got to his feet, remarking: 'That's a good horse, that one is! And I reckon it's about time he carried me home!' He left the room quietly, and they heard him clopping away down the drive!

There came a popping sound from the direction of the gentleman with the poltergeists, followed by another and another, as if small fireworks were exploding. He got up from the table and left, quite alone. There wasn't a sign of anything fussing about in his pockets and he seemed much calmer.

'Exactly!' murmured Miss Meadie half-aloud. 'I never did understand about poltergeists . . .'

The cavalier with the feathered hat was now a smartly dressed Member of Parliament. He said goodbye to Miss Meadie, explaining that he had to be in the House in the morning. The drowned lady was talking about sailing to someone who had looked very much like a pirate a few moments ago. They were arranging to sail round the world together. A tonsured monk was now a bishop, returning thanks for the meal they had all received, while a small grey lady left early, saying she had duties in the Public Library and would put Miss Meadie's books on psychic research on one side for her to collect in the morning.

The strangest transformation of all was William's skeleton. It had completely disappeared. By William's side was a charming young woman who was cuddling Harriet's baby. 'It is my baby,' she told Harriet. 'It always was. But you can come and play with it whenever you like.'

Harriet realized that this was for the best. A real live baby that everyone could interfere with was much less convenient than a phantom. Besides which, a real live baby would be even more enchanting to play with than a ghostling.

'Do you mind about your skeleton being a *her*?' she asked William.

'No,' he replied. 'If it can't be a skeleton I don't care what it is,' and he turned away.

The Rid-a-Ghoster was escaping through the door when several people prevented him, and took back their money. He did not even have enough left for his bus fare, and had to walk back to the town.

Harriet turned to Miss Meadie. She was feeling very guilty at the ways things had turned out. 'I'm terribly sorry,' she said. 'I seem to have taken away all your friends at once.'

Suddenly she noticed that Miss Meadie herself looked quite different from the Miss Meadie she had known before.

'It doesn't matter,' Miss Meadie said quietly. 'I was really getting tired of being a ghost myself. I'd rather be a human being. I'm going to have a home for cats and dogs that people have deserted. Goodnight, Harriet! I'm glad you won the bean. Come and see me sometimes, and I hope you enjoyed the party.'

And Harriet and William went home by bus, quite alone.

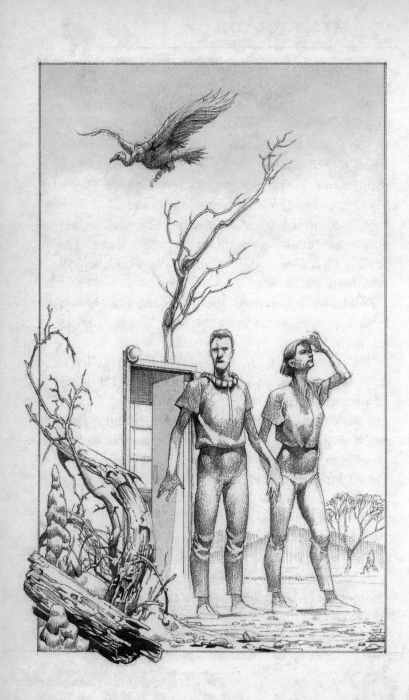

The Veldt

RAY BRADBURY

'George, I wish you'd look at the nursery.'
    'What's wrong with it?'
'I don't know.'
'Well, then.'
'I just want you to look at it, is all, or call a psychologist in to look at it.'
'What would a psychologist want with a nursery?'
'You know very well what he'd want.' His wife paused in the middle of the kitchen and watched the stove busy humming to itself, making supper for four.
'It's just that the nursery is different now than it was.'
'All right, let's have a look.'
They walked down the hall of their sound-proofed, Happy-life Home, which had cost them thirty thousand dollars to install, this house which clothed and fed and rocked them to sleep and played and sang and was

good to them. Their approach sensitized a switch some-where and the nursery light flicked on when they came within ten feet of it. Similarly, behind them, in the halls, lights went on and off as they left them behind, with a soft automaticity.

'Well,' said George Hadley.

They stood on the thatched floor of the nursery. It was forty feet across by forty feet long and thirty feet high; it had cost half as much again as the rest of the house. 'But nothing's too good for our children,' George had said.

The nursery was silent. It was empty as a jungle glade at hot high noon. The walls were blank and two-dimensional. Now, as George and Lydia Hadley stood in the centre of the room, the walls began to purr and recede into crystalline distance, it seemed, and presently an African veldt appeared, in three dimen-sions, on all sides, in colour, reproduced to the final pebble and bit of straw. The ceiling above them became a deep sky with a hot yellow sun.

George Hadley felt the perspiration start on his brow.

'Let's get out of this sun,' he said. 'This is a little too real. But I don't see anything wrong.'

'Wait a moment, you'll see,' said his wife.

Now the hidden odorophonics were beginning to blow a wind of odour at the two people in the middle of the baked veldtland. The hot straw smell of lion grass, the cool green smell of the hidden water-hole, the great rusty smell of animals, the smell of dust like a red paprika in the hot air. And now the sounds: the thump of distant antelope feet on grassy sod, the papery rustling of vultures. A shadow passed through the sky. The shadow flickered on George Hadley's upturned, sweating face.

'Filthy creatures,' he heard his wife say.

'The vultures.'

'You see, there are the lions, far over, that way. Now they're on their way to the water-hole. They've just been eating,' said Lydia. 'I don't know what.'

'Some animal.' George Hadley put his hand up to shield off the burning light from his squinted eyes. 'A zebra or a baby giraffe, maybe.'

'Are you *sure*?' His wife sounded peculiarly tense.

'No, it's a little late to be *sure*,' he said, amused. 'Nothing over there I can see but cleaned bone, and the vultures dropping for what's left.'

'Did you hear that scream?' she asked.

'No.'

'About a minute ago?'

'Sorry, no.'

The lions were coming. And again George Hadley was filled with admiration for the mechanical genius who had conceived this room. A miracle of efficiency selling for an absurdly low price. Every home should have one. Oh, occasionally they frightened you with their clinical accuracy, they startled you, gave you a twinge, but most of the time what fun for everyone, not only your own son and daughter but for yourself when you felt like a quick jaunt to a foreign land, a quick change of scenery. Well, here it was!

And here were the lions now, fifteen feet away, so real, so feverishly and startlingly real that you could feel the prickling fur on your hand, and your mouth was stuffed with the dusty upholstery smell of their heated pelts, and the yellow of them was in your eyes like the yellow of an exquisite French tapestry, the yellows of lions and summer grass, and the sound of the matted lion lungs exhaling on the silent noontide, and the smell of meat from the panting, dripping mouths.

The lions stood looking at George and Lydia Hadley with terrible green-yellow eyes.

'Watch out!' screamed Lydia.

The lions came running at them.

Lydia bolted and ran. Instinctively, George sprang after her. Outside, in the hall, with the door slammed, he was laughing and she was crying, and they both stood appalled at the other's reaction.

'George!'

'Lydia! Oh, my dear poor sweet Lydia!'

'They almost got us!'

'Walls, Lydia, remember; crystal walls, that's all they are. Oh, they look real, I must admit – Africa in your parlour – but it's all dimensional super-reactionary, super-sensitive colour film and mental tape film behind glass screens. It's all odorophonics and sonics, Lydia. Here's my handkerchief.'

'I'm afraid.' She came to him and put her body against him and cried steadily. 'Did you see? Did you feel? It's too real.'

'Now, Lydia . . .'

'You've got to tell Wendy and Peter not to read any more on Africa.'

'Of course – of course.' He patted her.

'Promise?'

'Sure.'

'And lock the nursery for a few days until I get my nerves settled.'

'You know how difficult Peter is about that. When I punished him a month ago by locking the nursery for even a few hours – the tantrum he threw! And Wendy too. They live for the nursery.'

'It's got to be locked, that's all there is to it.'

'All right.' Reluctantly he locked the huge door. 'You've been working too hard. You need a rest.'

'I don't know – I don't know,' she said, blowing her nose, and sitting down in a chair that immediately began to rock and comfort her. 'Maybe I don't have enough to do. Maybe I have time to think too much. Why don't we shut the whole house off for a few days and take a vacation?'

'You mean you want to fry my eggs for me?'

'Yes.' She nodded.

'And darn my socks?'

'Yes.' A frantic, watery-eyed nodding.

'And sweep the house?'

'Yes, yes – oh yes!'

'But I thought that's why we bought this house, so we wouldn't have to do anything?'

'That's just it. I feel like I don't belong here. The

97

house is wife and mother now and nursemaid. Can I compete with an African veldt? Can I give a bath and scrub the children as efficiently or quickly as the automatic scrub bath can? I cannot. And it isn't just me. It's you. You've been awfully nervous lately.'

'I suppose I have been smoking too much.'

'You look as if you didn't know what to do with yourself in this house, either. You smoke a little more every morning and drink a little more every afternoon and need a little more sedative every night. You're beginning to feel unnecessary too.'

'Am I?' He paused and tried to feel into himself to see what was really there.

'Oh, George!' She looked beyond him, at the nursery door. 'Those lions can't get out of there, can they?'

He looked at the door and saw it tremble as if something had jumped against it from the other side.

'Of course not,' he said.

At dinner they ate alone, for Wendy and Peter were at a special plastic carnival across town and had televised home to say they'd be late, to go ahead eating. So George Hadley, bemused, sat watching the dining-room table produce warm dishes of food from its mechanical interior.

'We forgot the ketchup,' he said.

'Sorry,' said a small voice within the table, and ketchup appeared.

As for the nursery, thought George Hadley, it won't

hurt for the children to be locked out of it a while. Too much of anything isn't good for anyone. And it was clearly indicated that the children had been spending a little too much time on Africa. That *sun*. He could feel it on his neck, still, like a hot paw. And the *lions*. And the smell of blood. Remarkable how the nursery caught the telepathic emanations of the children's minds and created life to fill their every desire. The children thought lions, and there were lions. The children thought zebras, and there were zebras. Sun – sun. Giraffes – giraffes. Death and death.

That *last*. He chewed tastelessly on the meat that the table had cut for him. Death thoughts. They were awfully young, Wendy and Peter, for death thoughts. Or, no, you were never too young, really. Long before you knew what death was you were wishing it on someone else. When you were two years old you were shooting people with cap pistols.

But this – the long, hot African veldt – the awful death in the jaws of a lion. And repeated again and again.

'Where are you going?'

He didn't answer Lydia. Preoccupied, he let the lights glow softly on ahead of him, extinguish behind him as he padded to the nursery door. He listened against it. Far away, a lion roared.

He unlocked the door and opened it. Just before he stepped inside, he heard a far-away scream. And then another roar from the lions, which subsided quickly.

He stepped into Africa. How many times in the last

year had he opened this door and found Wonderland, Alice, the Mock Turtle, or Aladdin and his Magical Lamp, or Jack Pumpkinhead of Oz, or Dr Dolittle, or the cow jumping over a very real-appearing moon – all the delightful contraptions of a make-believe world. How often had he seen Pegasus flying in the sky ceiling, or seen fountains of red fireworks, or heard angel voices singing. But now, this yellow hot Africa, this bake oven with murder in the heat. Perhaps Lydia was right. Perhaps they needed a little vacation from the fantasy which was growing a bit too real for ten-year-old children. It was all right to exercise one's mind with gymnastic fantasies, but when the lively child mind settled on one pattern . . .? It seemed that, at a distance, for the past month, he had heard lions roaring, and smelled their strong odour seeping as far away as his study door. But, being busy, he had paid it no attention.

George Hadley stood on the African grassland alone. The lions looked up from their feeding, watching him. The only flaw to the illusion was the open door through which he could see his wife, far down the dark hall, like a framed picture, eating her dinner abstractedly.

'Go away,' he said to the lions.

They did not go.

He knew the principle of the room exactly. You sent out your thoughts. Whatever you thought would appear.

'Let's have Aladdin and his lamp,' he snapped.

The veldtland remained, the lions remained.

'Come on, room! I demand Aladdin!' he said.

Nothing happened. The lions mumbled in their baked pelts.

'Aladdin!'

He went back to dinner. 'The fool room's out of order,' he said. 'It won't respond.'

'Or –'

'Or what?'

'Or it *can't* respond,' said Lydia, 'because the children have thought about Africa and lions and killing so many days that the room's in a rut.'

'Could be.'

'Or Peter's set it to remain that way.'

'*Set* it?'

'He may have got into the machinery and fixed something.'

'Peter doesn't know machinery.'

'He's a wise one for ten. That IQ of his –'

'Nevertheless –'

'Hello, Mum. Hello, Dad.'

The Hadleys turned. Wendy and Peter were coming in the front door, cheeks like peppermint candy, eyes like bright blue agate marbles, a smell of ozone on their jumpers from their trip in the helicopter.

'You're just in time for supper,' said both parents.

'We're full of strawberry ice-cream and hot dogs,' said the children, holding hands. 'But we'll sit and watch.'

'Yes, come tell us about the nursery,' said George Hadley.

The brother and sister blinked at him and then at each other. 'Nursery?'

'All about Africa and everything,' said the father with false joviality.

'I don't understand,' said Peter.

'Your mother and I were just travelling through Africa with rod and reel; Tom Swift and his Electric Lion,' said George Hadley.

'There's no Africa in the nursery,' said Peter simply.

'Oh, come now, Peter. We know better.'

'I don't remember any Africa,' said Peter to Wendy. 'Do you?'

'No.'

'Run see and come tell.'

She obeyed.

'Wendy, come back here!' said George Hadley, but she was gone. The house lights followed her like a flock of fireflies. Too late, he realized he had forgotten to lock the nursery door after his last inspection.

'Wendy'll look and come tell us,' said Peter.

'She doesn't have to tell *me*. I've seen it.'

'I'm sure you're mistaken, Father.'

'I'm not, Peter. Come along now.'

But Wendy was back. 'It's not Africa,' she said breathlessly.

'We'll see about this,' said George Hadley, and they all walked down the hall together and opened the nursery door.

There was a green, lovely forest, a lovely river, a

purple mountain, high voices singing, and Rima, lovely and mysterious, lurking in the trees with colourful flights of butterflies, like animated bouquets, lingering in her long hair. The African veldtland was gone. The lions were gone. Only Rima was here now, singing a song so beautiful that it brought tears to your eyes.

George Hadley looked in at the changed scene. 'Go to bed,' he said to the children.

They opened their mouths.

'You heard me,' he said.

They went off to the air closet, where a wind sucked them like brown leaves up the flue to their slumber rooms.

George Hadley walked through the singing glade and picked up something that lay in the corner near where the lions had been. He walked slowly back to his wife.

'What is that?' she asked.

'An old wallet of mine,' he said.

He showed it to her. The smell of hot grass was on it and the smell of a lion. There were drops of saliva on it, it had been chewed, and there were blood smears on both sides.

He closed the nursery door and locked it, tight.

In the middle of the night he was still awake and he knew his wife was awake. 'Do you think Wendy changed it?' she said at last, in the dark room.

'Of course.'

'Made it from a veldt into a forest and put Rima there instead of lions?'

'Yes.'

'Why?'

'I don't know. But it's staying locked until I find out.'

'How did your wallet get there?'

'I don't know anything,' he said, 'except that I'm beginning to be sorry we bought that room for the children. If children are neurotic at all, a room like that –'

'It's supposed to help them work off their neuroses in a healthful way.'

'I'm starting to wonder.' He stared at the ceiling.

'We've given the children everything they ever wanted. Is this our reward – secrecy, disobedience?'

'Who was it said, "Children are carpets, they should be stepped on occasionally"? We've never lifted a hand. They're insufferable – let's admit it. They come and go when they like; they treat us as if *we* were offspring. They're spoiled and we're spoiled.'

'They've been acting funny ever since you forbade them to take the rocket to New York a few months ago.'

'They're not old enough to do that alone, I explained.'

'Nevertheless, I've noticed they've been decidedly cool towards us since.'

'I think I'll have David McClean come tomorrow morning to have a look at Africa.'

'But it's not Africa now, it's Green Mansions country and Rima.'

'I have a feeling it'll be Africa again before then.'

A moment later they heard the screams.

Two screams. Two people screaming from down-stairs. And then a roar of lions.

'Wendy and Peter aren't in their rooms,' said his wife.

He lay in his bed with his beating heart. 'No,' he said. 'They've broken into the nursery.'

'Those screams – they sound familiar.'

'Do they?'

'Yes, awfully.'

And although their beds tried very hard, the two adults couldn't be rocked to sleep for another hour. A smell of cats was in the night air.

'Father?' said Peter.

'Yes.'

Peter looked at his shoes. He never looked at his father any more, nor at his mother. 'You aren't going to lock up the nursery for good, are you?'

'That all depends.'

'On what?' snapped Peter.

'On you and your sister. If you intersperse this Africa with a little variety – oh, Sweden, perhaps, or Denmark or China –'

'I thought we were free to play as we wished.'

'You are, within reasonable bounds.'

'What's wrong with Africa, Father?'

'Oh, so now you admit you have been conjuring up Africa, do you?'

'I wouldn't want the nursery locked up,' said Peter coldly. 'Ever.'

'Matter of fact, we're thinking of turning the whole house off for about a month. Live sort of a carefree one-for-all existence.'

'That sounds dreadful! Would I have to tie my own shoes instead of letting the shoe-tier do it? And brush my own teeth and comb my hair and give myself a bath?'

'It would be fun for a change, don't you think?'

'No, it would be horrid. I didn't like it when you took out the picture painter last month.'

'That's because I wanted you to learn to paint all by yourself, son.'

'I don't want to do anything but look and listen and smell; what else is there to do?'

'All right, go play in Africa.'

'Will you shut off the house sometime soon?'

'We're considering it.'

'I don't think you'd better consider it any more, Father.'

'I won't have any threats from my son!'

'Very well.' And Peter strolled off to the nursery.

'Am I on time?' said David McClean.

'Breakfast?' asked George Hadley.

'Thanks, had some. What's the trouble?'

'David, you're a psychologist.'

'I should hope so.'

'Well, then, have a look at our nursery. You saw it a year ago when you dropped by; did you notice anything peculiar about it then?'

'Can't say I did; the usual violences, a tendency towards a slight paranoia here or there, usual in children because they feel persecuted by parents constantly, but, oh, really nothing.'

They walked down the hall. 'I locked the nursery up,' explained the father, 'and the children broke back into it during the night. I let them stay so they could form the patterns for you to see.'

There was a terrible screaming from the nursery.

'There it is,' said George Hadley. 'See what you make of it.'

They walked in on the children without rapping.

The screams had faded. The lions were feeding.

'Run outside a moment, children,' said George Hadley. 'No, don't change the mental combination. Leave the walls as they are. Get!'

With the children gone, the two men stood studying the lions clustered at a distance, eating with great relish whatever it was they had caught.

'I wish I knew what it was,' said George Hadley. 'Sometimes I can almost see. Do you think if I brought high-powered binoculars here and –'

David McClean laughed dryly. 'Hardly.' He turned to study all four walls. 'How long has this been going on?'

'A little over a month.'

'It certainly doesn't feel good.'

'I want facts, not feelings.'

'My dear George, a psychologist never saw a fact in his life. He only hears about feelings; vague things. This doesn't feel good, I tell you. Trust my hunches and my instincts, I have a nose for something bad. This is very bad. My advice to you is to have the whole damn room torn down and your children brought to me every day during the next year for treatment.'

'Is it that bad?'

'I'm afraid so. One of the original uses of these nurseries was so that we could study the patterns left on the walls by the child's mind, study at our leisure, and help the child. In this case, however, the room has become a channel towards — destructive thoughts, instead of a release away from them.'

'Didn't you sense this before?'

'I sensed only that you had spoiled your children more than most. And now you're letting them down in some way. What way?'

'I wouldn't let them go to New York.'

'What else?'

'I've taken a few machines from the house and threatened them, a month ago, with closing up the nursery unless they did their homework. I did close it for a few days to show I meant business.'

'Aha!'

'Does that mean anything?'

'Everything. Where before they had a Santa Claus now they have a Scrooge. Children prefer Santas. You've let this room and this house replace you and your wife in your children's affections. This room is their mother and father, far more important in their lives than their real parents. And now you come along and want to shut it off. No wonder there's hatred here. You can feel it

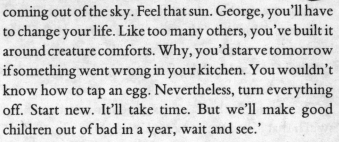

coming out of the sky. Feel that sun. George, you'll have to change your life. Like too many others, you've built it around creature comforts. Why, you'd starve tomorrow if something went wrong in your kitchen. You wouldn't know how to tap an egg. Nevertheless, turn everything off. Start new. It'll take time. But we'll make good children out of bad in a year, wait and see.'

'But won't the shock be too much for the children, shutting the room up abruptly, for good?'

'I don't want them going any deeper into this, that's all.'

The lions were finished with their red feast.

The lions were standing on the edge of the clearing watching the two men.

'Now *I'm* feeling persecuted,' said McClean. 'Let's get out of here. I never have cared for these damned rooms. Make me nervous.'

'The lions look real, don't they?' said George Hadley. 'I don't suppose there's any way –'

'What?'

'– that they could *become* real?'

'Not that I know.'

'Some flaw in the machinery, a tampering or something?'

'No.'

They went to the door.

'I don't imagine the room will like being turned off,' said the father.

'Nothing ever likes to die – even a room.'

'I wonder if it hates me for wanting to switch it off?'

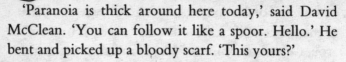

'Paranoia is thick around here today,' said David McClean. 'You can follow it like a spoor. Hello.' He bent and picked up a bloody scarf. 'This yours?'

'No.' George Hadley's face was rigid. 'It belongs to Lydia.'

They went to the fuse-box together and threw the switch that killed the nursery.

The two children were in hysterics. They screamed and pranced and threw things. They yelled and sobbed and swore and jumped at the furniture.

'You can't do that to the nursery, you can't!'

'Now, children.'

The children flung themselves on to a couch, weeping.

'George,' said Lydia Hadley, 'turn on the nursery, just for a few moments. You can't be so abrupt.'

'No.'

'You can't be so cruel.'

'Lydia, it's off, and it stays off. And the whole damn house dies as of here and now. The more I see of the mess we've put ourselves in, the more it sickens me. We've been contemplating our mechanical, electronic navels for too long. My God, how we need a breath of honest air!'

And he marched about the house turning off the voice clocks, the stoves, the heaters, the shoe-shiners, the shoe-lacers, the body-scrubbers and swabbers and massagers, and every other machine he could put his hand to.

The house was full of dead bodies, it seemed. It felt like a mechanical cemetery. So silent. None of the humming hidden energy of machines waiting to function at the tap of a button.

'Don't let them do it!' wailed Peter at the ceiling, as if he was talking to the house, the nursery. 'Don't let Father kill everything.' He turned to his father. 'Oh, I hate you!'

'Insults won't get you anywhere.'

'I wish you were dead!'

'We were, for a long while. Now we're going to really start living. Instead of being handled and massaged, we're going to live.'

Wendy was still crying and Peter joined her again. 'Just a moment, just one moment, just another moment of nursery,' they wailed.

'Oh, George,' said the wife, 'it can't hurt.'

'All right — all right, if they'll only just shut up. One minute, mind you, and then off for ever.'

'Daddy, Daddy, Daddy!' sang the children, smiling with wet faces.

'And then we're going on a vacation. David Mc-Clean is coming back in half an hour to help us move out and get to the airport. I'm going to dress. You turn the nursery on for a minute, Lydia, just a minute, mind you.'

And the three of them went babbling off while he let himself be vacuumed upstairs through the air flue and set about dressing himself. A minute later Lydia appeared.

'I'll be glad when we get away,' she sighed.

'Did you leave them in the nursery?'

'I wanted to dress too. Oh, that horrid Africa. What can they see in it?'

'Well, in five minutes we'll be on our way to Iowa. Lord, how did we ever get in this house? What prompted us to buy a nightmare?'

'Pride, money, foolishness.'

'I think we'd better get downstairs before those kids get engrossed with those damned beasts again.'

Just then they heard the children calling, 'Daddy, Mummy, come quick – quick!'

They went downstairs in the air flue and ran down the hall. The children were nowhere in sight. 'Wendy? Peter!'

They ran into the nursery. The veldtland was empty save for the lions waiting, looking at them. 'Peter, Wendy?'

The door slammed.

'Wendy, Peter!'

George Hadley and his wife whirled and ran back to the door.

'Open the door!' cried George Hadley, trying the knob. 'Why, they've locked it from the outside! Peter!' He beat at the door. 'Open up!'

He heard Peter's voice outside, against the door.

'Don't let them switch off the nursery and the house,' he was saying.

Mr and Mrs George Hadley beat at the door. 'Now, don't be ridiculous, children. It's time to go. Mr Mc-Clean'll be here in a minute and . . .'

And then they heard the sounds.

The lions on three sides of them, in the yellow veldt grass, padding through the dry straw, rumbling and roaring in their throats.

The lions.

Mr Hadley looked at his wife and they turned and looked back at the beasts edging slowly forward, crouching, tails stiff.

Mr and Mrs Hadley screamed.

And suddenly they realized why those other screams had sounded familiar.

'Well, here I am,' said David McClean in the nursery doorway. 'Oh, hello.' He stared at the two children seated in the centre of the open glade eating a little picnic lunch. Beyond them was the water-hole and the yellow veldtland; above was the hot sun. He began to perspire. 'Where are your father and mother?'

The children looked up and smiled. 'Oh, they'll be here directly.'

'Good, we must get going.' At a distance Mr McClean saw the lions fighting and clawing and then quieting down to feed in silence under the shady trees.

He squinted at the lions with his hand up to his eyes.

Now the lions were done feeding. They moved to the water-hole to drink.

A shadow flickered over Mr McClean's hot face. Many shadows flickered. The vultures were dropping down the blazing sky.

'A cup of tea?' asked Wendy in the silence.

Goosey Goosey Gander

ANN PILLING

The Bostocks were moving from the pretty Lancashire village of Brampton to a house slap-bang in the middle of the town, and Lawrence and Julia didn't like it one bit.

Julia was ten, and had lots of friends at her primary school. Why go and buy a house miles away in horrible, dirty Darnley-in-Makerfield? You couldn't hear the birds sing there because of all the factory noises, and you had to keep your eyes peeled wherever you went, for fear of walking under a bus. 'It's not *fair*,' she pouted, watching her mother wrap up china in newspaper and pack it in cardboard boxes. 'I hate the new house.'

'I hate it too,' said Lawrence. He was five and he always copied what Julia said. Secretly though, he felt rather excited about moving. It meant he would go to school at last, and he'd been promised his own bedroom too. In the cottage he had to share with Julia. Besides, Great-aunt Annie was already living at the new house and Great-aunt Annie had a sweet tin.

'You can't hate what you've never seen,' Mrs Bostock said wearily. 'Dad's offered to take you to see Baillie Square half a dozen times now it's all been redecorated, but you just won't go.'

'Well, I still don't think it's fair,' moaned Julia. 'I like the country. Darnley's dirty, and it smells.'

Her mother abandoned her china-wrapping and sat down on the floor. 'Listen,' she said. 'First of all, Darnley doesn't smell, and 19 Baillie Square is a beautiful house. It's all been cleaned up and the factories aren't allowed to have smoking chimneys any more.'

'But I won't have any *friends*. People don't live in places like Baillie Square, right in the middle of towns.'

'That's not true either. There are the Wilkinsons two doors away, and the Shaws just opposite, and the three Vicarage children on the corner . . .'

'Yuk! That's another thing, Aunt Annie'll make us go to church. She's church mad.'

'Remember what the doctor told Dad,' Mrs Bostock reminded her. She'd gone beyond the red-faced arguey stage now and looked all set to burst into tears. 'He ought to give up the long drive into work. It's miles from here to his office, love, and when there's a hold-up on the motorway . . .'

'But why couldn't we just buy somewhere nearer, in another village? Why Darnley? Ugh!' and Julia did cry now.

'Well, it's only an experiment. We're not buying the house from Aunt Annie yet. We're just renting part of it, and if it doesn't work out we can come back here, to Sweet Briars. Dad's only letting the Jacksons use it for a year.'

A year. It felt like for ever to Julia. 'Some experiment!' she said rudely, glaring at all the packing cases. 'I'm going to see Charlotte. It'll probably be my last chance,' and she stormed off.

Lawrence cuddled up to his mother. He didn't like it when Julia shouted. 'Is there a fire station at Aunt Annie's?' he said timidly.

Mrs Bostock hesitated. Just before Christmas he'd managed to find some matches and started a blaze in the garage. Two fire-engines had come over from Headingford and he'd been fascinated by them. He'd not understood that he could have burned Sweet Briars to the ground, only that two gleaming red trucks and eight men with shiny yellow hats had come tearing up their lane. And all because of him. Since then all matches had been kept hidden. But Lawrence was still fascinated by fire. Only last week they'd caught him fiddling with a cigarette-lighter.

'There'll be one in Manchester,' she said cautiously. 'That's a very big city. We could go there on the bus. There are lots of shops in Manchester, and cinemas, and a skating-rink, and there's a famous orchestra called the Hallé.'

But his glassy eyes told her that he'd not heard one word about Manchester. All he cared about was living near the fire station.

★

'I can smell something burning,' Dad said. 'Have you left the milk pan on, Auntie?' It was eleven o'clock and Mr and Mrs Bostock were having a late night drink down in the basement flat. Julia was there too. Her official bedtime was eight-thirty, but she came down most evenings complaining that she couldn't sleep. She'd started off in the big back attic, next to Lawrence, but that had only lasted a week. Her bedroom was on the floor below now, next to Mum and Dad. She said she felt 'safer' there.

'Safe from what?' Dad had said rather grumpily, watching Mum trying to manoeuvre a mattress down the narrow attic stairs. He wasn't allowed to lift heavy things, since his illness.

Julia wouldn't tell, except that she thought Aunt Annie's had a 'creepy feeling'.

'Stuff and nonsense. It's a lovely old house.'

Great-aunt Annie was eighty-one. She was still very fit but she did get muddled about things. 'It'll be them students,' she said, as Dad went to investigate the smell. 'They're up at all hours, cooking.' The Bostocks exchanged glances. Four students from the Polytechnic had rented rooms at 19 Baillie Square last year but they'd left months ago.

'I'll just go up and check in our kitchen then, Auntie,' Dad said. 'There's certainly nothing on in yours.' And he climbed the stairs to the ground floor. Mum and Julia followed and they all stood together in the long narrow hall with its pattern of black and white tiles, tiles that had been washed morning and evening years ago, by a little servant girl, according to Aunt Annie. She'd been born in the house, and her father before her.

The smell was stronger here. Julia ran into the front room where they'd had a fire burning in the grate. But nothing remained of it except a heap of reddish ash and anyhow, the big fire-guard was firmly in position.

'It's upstairs,' Mum said, turning very pale all of a sudden. 'It's . . . *Lawrence!*' And she began to mount the staircase, two steps at a time.

Julia shoved past and was in the attic before her mother had reached the second-floor landing. Dad, who wasn't supposed to rush anywhere, made his way up more slowly.

'Well there's nothing burning,' Julia said, coming out of the tiny back bedroom. 'It's all OK in here, and Loll's fast asleep.'

Nothing could be seen of Lawrence except a little mound of bedding. The room smelt of fresh paint and wallpaper but the scorching, burning smell was much stronger now.

'There must be a big fire in town,' Dad said, puffing slightly as he appeared at the top of the stairs. 'I didn't hear any sirens though.'

'Well, Loll must have because he's *not* in this bed.' Julia had deliberately sat down right in the middle of the hump, just to annoy him, and discovered it was empty.

Mrs Bostock tore back the covers. All she found

was a collection of stuffed toys, half a biscuit and an old comic. He wasn't in the attic and he wasn't in the rooms down below. Loll had vanished into thin air.

Back in the hall Dad pulled open the heavy front door and looked out. A small five-year-old surely couldn't have climbed up, unbolted it and slipped through, yet he was starting to panic. Loll was drawn to fires like ducks were to water.

As he stood staring up and down the street Great-aunt Annie suddenly rapped on her basement window. Dad looked down the grating in the pavement and saw her smiling, and pointing at something. She'd got Loll in her arms, wrapped up in a blanket, and he was waving a picture book.

'*Lawrence!*' Dad went back inside and took the phone off Mum. She was nearly in tears now, and in the middle of dialling 999. 'It's OK,' he said. 'He was with Aunt Annie. Don't know how on earth he slipped past us.'

'Perhaps he was in that little loo on the second floor landing,' she sniffed. 'He likes that game. I never thought of . . .'

'No he wasn't,' Julia interrupted. 'I looked in there.'

'Now come on, Loll, this is naughty. You're keeping Aunt Annie out of bed.' Down in the basement sitting-room Dad took him into his arms, restored the tatty nursery rhyme book to its shelf and went to the door. 'I'm sorry, Auntie. This won't happen again.'

'It's all right, chuck, I don't mind. I wasn't in bed any road.'

But Lawrence had started to howl. 'I want to see the lady again, I want to show you that *lady*.'

'Tomorrow. You can come down for a story tomorrow. Listen, we should all be in bed by now, it's nearly midnight.'

'But what about that smell?' Julia started, the minute Aunt Annie's door was closed. Mum, following her up the basement stairs, gave her a sharp dig in the back.

'It was obviously outside,' she whispered. 'It's gone now anyhow. Listen, let's just keep quiet about it. I think Loll's getting over that fire thing so the less said at this stage the better.'

Dad was making his way upstairs to put Lawrence back in bed and Julia was following, with her mother. But at the part where the stairs widened out, on the first landing, she suddenly stopped dead.

'Come on, Julia, for Heaven's sake. I'm tired. What are you doing?'

'I don't like going past here at night, Mum. This is the creepy part.'

'Darling, it's not a bit "creepy". You love Aunt Annie's old rocking-horse don't you? And it's just the place for it on this landing, much better than where it used to be, in that poky back room.' But she'd noticed that Julia never sat on the old black horse now, or threaded ribbons through its mane like she used to.

'I get a funny cold feeling when I go past this bit,' she said in an embarrassed rush, grabbing at her mother's hand. 'You can say I'm silly, Mum, but I *do*.

And I wish we could go back to Sweet Briars like you promised. I don't want to stay here for a whole year, I just *don't!*' And she ran into her bedroom and slammed the door.

Gradually, though, Julia stopped complaining about living at Aunt Annie's. Nearly all the children in the square went to her school and they fell over themselves to be friendly when they knew she was the great-niece of old Annie Birdsall. She'd been on telly last year, on *Look North*. It was her eightieth birthday and they'd had her talking about her house in Baillie Square. Her grandfather had bought it when it was brand-new and the Birdsall family had lived in it ever since.

Lawrence loved school. It was nearly all play for the infants and at twelve o'clock Mum took him home for dinner and a little sleep. On his very first Friday he got a book out of the story box called *Our Friend the Fireman*.

Mum frowned when she saw it. She really thought Loll was getting over his fascination with fires but that night she realized she was wrong. There was a sudden terrific smell of burning in the house as she stood in the kitchen, drying the bedtime mugs before going upstairs. All the windows were closed and there'd definitely been no sirens in the street. This time she ran down to Aunt Annie's flat first. The old lady was nodding in her chair, making gentle snoring noises. No fumes down here though, no smoke, no smell, *no Loll*. Mrs Bostock tore up through the house, flinging all the doors open as she went. Her husband was already asleep in the large front bedroom. Julia was asleep, too. There was nothing burning in the back attic though she kicked aside all the empty boxes they'd stored in there, just to make sure, and Lawrence's room was in perfect order for once. She'd given it a good clean-up while he'd been playing in the square that afternoon, with Julia and her new friends.

Even so, she tugged the wobbly old wardrobe away from the wall and looked behind it, pulled out drawers, and ripped back a bit of the carpet in case the floor-boards were smouldering, the smell in the room was so overpowering. *Nothing*. But when she turned Lawrence's covers back, to check that he was safe under his usual mound, she found the bed empty. It was just like the first time.

Instinct told her that he'd somehow slipped past and gone down to see Aunt Annie again. The big attraction was her sweet tin and all her old-fashioned picture books. Since the move Mr and Mrs Bostock hadn't had much time for reading to Lawrence, but Great-aunt Annie had all the time in the world. She loved children. Julia got a bit irritated when she repeated all the old Baillie Square stories, and she didn't much like being told to 'say your prayers' every night. Loll didn't mind though. He said little prayers with Auntie Annie, after his story and his sweet.

When Mrs Bostock got down to the basement again she was out of breath. There were fifty-six stairs between Loll's door and Aunt Annie's and she'd run down every one of them. There he was, sitting on his aunt's knee, with the little ginger cat on *his* knee, and they were all looking at nursery rhymes.

> 'Goosey goosey gander,
> Whither shall I wander?
> Upstairs and downstairs
> And in my lady's chamber . . .'

'That lady, Auntie, *that* lady,' he was jabbering excitedly. 'That one in the funny hat . . .'

When she saw Mrs Bostock Great-aunt Annie looked slightly guilty. 'I'm sorry, chuck,' she said, 'but he just came down, all on his own, and I thought one little story wouldn't hurt, to settle him like.'

'It was a lady brought me,' Lawrence said sleepily, yawning and sticking a thumb in his mouth.

'It's a funny hat isn't it, Loll? Just like a pair of frilly knickers put on upside down.' Great-aunt Annie giggled. 'Everyone used to wear them caps in the old days, everyone in service.'

'What's that she's got?' Lawrence was as well-practised as Julia in spinning out bedtime and he'd turned back to Goosey Goosey Gander.

'It's a candlestick, chuck. In the olden days, when there was no electricity . . .'

'Good *night*, Aunt Annie,' Mrs Bostock said firmly, shooing Loll up the stairs. She didn't want him falling asleep thinking about candles and striking matches.

That night she put a spare mattress on Julia's floor and he slept on it. The strong scorching, burning smell had evaporated as quickly as it had come but unless there was a fire in the town there was obviously some problem with the electrics in this old house, and that was dangerous. In the morning she'd ask Mrs Watkins over at the Vicarage for the name of an electrician. The wiring ought to be inspected for faults.

When Loll was asleep she went downstairs one last time to check round. As she climbed back upstairs the great black horse loomed up at her out of the darkness, stopping her in her tracks. There *was* a kind of coldness on this landing, but it was probably an ill-fitting window, or a damp wall. Even so, she shivered slightly as she stood there, thinking how Julia had grabbed at her hand.

The night it happened Mum and Dad were out at a special dinner in the Town Hall. Aunt Annie was 'baby-sitting', not that she had anything to do. Julia always put herself to bed and she got Loll organized too. They weren't *babies*.

At half past ten, just before she had her milky drink, Great-aunt Annie came all the way up to the top of the house to say good night to them both. Julia was amazed. Surely she couldn't manage the steep attic stairs on those stumpy little legs of hers?

But she did. Julia heard 'Good night, chuck,' and Loll's door being pulled shut. Then there was a kind of heavy thud. She was puzzled. Great-aunt Annie was quite fat but it wasn't the repeated thudding of someone lumbering down bare wooden stairs, just one big thud, then silence.

She forgot all about it in the embarrassment of the good night kiss. The old lady waddled across the room and thrust a slightly prickly cheek up against Julia's. 'Night, night, chuck. Have you said your prayers?' She hadn't, of course, but if she confessed Aunt Annie might kneel down and start praying there and then.

'Good night, Auntie,' she said sleepily and ducked smartly under the covers, just in case another kiss was on its way.

The church clock woke her, St Christopher's on the other side of the square, striking one. She sat up in bed and looked through the window. In the broad cobbled lane that ran along the backs of the houses there were spaces for people's cars but theirs was empty. Her parents must still be at the Town Hall.

She was trying to get back to sleep when she smelt the burning. She sat up again, pushed the window open and sniffed. It was a definite city smell, car fumes and factories and dogs, not fresh like the country. But there was no smell of fire. This smell was coming from *inside* the house, like the other times.

She ran into her parents' bedroom and switched on the light. Nothing amiss in here, just Mum's jeans hung neatly over a chair and Dad's clothes in a heap on the floor. He was messy like Loll. She and Mum were the two tidy ones.

Loll. Mum thought he was over his fire thing, but Julia wasn't so sure and she began to climb the attic stairs. Every single Friday he brought the Fireman book home from school. They all knew it off by heart. He was stuck on two things, that book and Goosey Goosey Gander in Aunt Annie's collection. His favourite picture was the girl in the knicker hat looking into dusty corners with her candlestick. 'My lady!' he shouted, whenever they got to that page.

When she reached the top of the stairs Julia stopped stone dead. Mum always left Loll's door open at night but Aunt Annie had closed it and now it wouldn't open again. She wrenched at the handle and pushed and kicked and yelled, but something heavy had fallen against the door from the inside. She hurled herself at it bodily, making it move a fraction of an inch, and through the crack smoke came curling, thick grey smoke that got thicker and darker by the second. 'Loll!' she screamed, then *'Lawrence!'* And through the crack she heard his voice, tight and high with terror, 'Julia!'

The nearest phone was in their kitchen. She almost fell down the attic steps then started on the main stairs. They were splintery and cold to her bare feet. As she reached the rocking-horse landing she drew a deep breath. She'd never, ever, come as far down as this so late at night and, as she hurled herself past, the cold rushed out at her, just as if she'd opened a freezer cabinet. The flaring wooden nostrils of the great black wooden charger breathed winter, turning the inside air to ice.

As she picked up the kitchen phone she thought of that strange thud, just before Aunt Annie's whiskery goodnight kiss. Now she knew what it was. The electricians were going to start rewiring next week and they'd been humping all the furniture about in the attics. Aunt Annie must have banged too hard when she shut the door. That wobbly old wardrobe must have fallen against it.

Julie heard herself telling the man on the other end of the phone that the fire was at 19 Baillie Square *and would they please hurry*. A child was trapped and she couldn't get the door open, and her aunt was old and her mum and dad still at the Town Hall. Her cool calm voice didn't sound a bit like her normal one. She felt separated from that cool-headed grown-up Julia by a thick wall of glass.

'*Julia!*' Loll's shrill scream of terror rang again in her ears.

'They'll be with you in a minute, love,' the man on the phone said calmly, *but a minute might be too late*. She scrabbled under the sink, found Dad's big hammer and made her way back upstairs. She'd once seen someone smash a door in with a hammer on TV. If she could make a big enough hole in one of the panels she could climb through and pull Loll out. He was only little.

She'd just reached the rocking-horse landing when she heard a voice in the hall. 'Auntie Annie's gone to sleep,' it said blearily. 'You read it to me, Julia, I want to see my *lady*.' She spun round and almost fell back down the stairs. Lawrence was standing on the black and white tiles, his eyes still gummed up as if he'd been roused from a very deep sleep, the old nursery rhyme book thrust out hopefully towards her.

She'd not even reached him when there was a great hammering on the front door. 'S'cuse me, love,' three firemen shoved past and pelted up the stairs. Outside they could see three more, uncoiling a flat white hose, and a ladder was being unfolded in gleaming sections and propped against the house. Loll dropped his book and crept out on to the front door step, his eyes shining. 'Now then, back inside, little feller, you'll catch your death out here,' and a policeman was sweeping him up in his arms and carrying him into the kitchen.

Quite suddenly, Mum and Dad were there too. Mum had her arms round Julia, telling her she was a brave, sensible girl who deserved a medal. Dad, who'd been down to check on Aunt Annie and found her peacefully asleep, was asking the fireman what was happening upstairs. Mum had forbidden him to go rushing about, because of his illness.

'Panic over,' someone said a few minutes later, coming downstairs. 'Sorry about all the water, sir. It always makes the biggest mess.' His hands and face were black and he'd left big splodgy footprints all over the bare boards. 'The blaze is out anyhow. It was in the eaves cupboard, just a load of old newspapers. Must have been there for years, from the look of them.'

'How did it happen, though?' Mum said. She wanted to cuddle Loll but he seemed quite happy with the policeman.

'Old wiring, from the look of it. It all needs ripping out, I'd say. Half the house fires we get are electrical. Good job there was nobody sleeping in that room. An old wardrobe had fallen against the door. It could have been a death trap.'

'But someone does sleep in there. Loll, our little boy . . .'

'He'd gone down to see Aunt Annie as usual,' Julia said firmly. 'He wasn't there when the fire started.'

But he was. She'd heard him screaming on the other side of the door. How on earth had he escaped from that blazing attic? She'd not seen him slip past.

'It was the *lady*,' Lawrence said sleepily, finding Goosey Gander in his book, to show the policeman. 'She took me to see Aunt Annie, she takes me lots of nights. But Auntie was asleep,' he added reproachfully, 'and I've not had my sweet.'

Dad was sitting on a kitchen stool with Julia on his knee. Now the fire was out and Loll was safe she'd started to shiver. 'Your feet are cold,' her father said, chafing them with his big comforting hands. 'No wonder, walking up and down those stairs. I really must give the carpet people another ring, you've got some nasty splinters. And I'm getting another electrical firm in tomorrow, Mary. Harrisons should never have left the attic in that state. I feel like suing them.'

'This little chap's as warm as toast,' the policeman said suddenly. '*His* feet aren't cold, and I can't see any splinters. Funny that, when he's been running up and down the bare boards,' and he handed him back to his mother. It was true, Loll's feet felt like two tiny hot water bottles all pink and clean from his bath, not grimy and grey like Julia's. It was just as if someone had scooped him up from his bed, before the fire took hold, and carried him gently down to safety, so gently he'd hardly woken up.

As the last of the firemen shut the front door something rolled into a corner. Julia, who was wide awake now and looking forward to milk and biscuits before she went back to bed, bent down and picked it up. 'Where's this come from?' she said, taking the old bent candlestick and putting it on the kitchen table. Her mother shrugged. 'I don't know. I've never seen it before. Perhaps Aunt Annie put it out for St Christopher's jumble sale last week. I could polish that up. It's brass.'

Before the new electricians did the rewiring the attics were cleared out completely. Lawrence slept with Julia and although he'd loved his tiny room under the roof he didn't argue. It was all black now and it had a horrid burny smell still. The lady didn't like it either. She never came to see him any more, or carried him down to Aunt Annie.

The fireman had dumped the old newspapers in the middle of the floor and hosed them down. Dad, anxious to rescue what he could, went through the remains very carefully. Old papers fascinated him, and these were all local.

One rainy Sunday afternoon he looked up from the

kitchen table, where he'd been piecing them together, and handed something to Mum. 'Read that,' he said, and his voice was strangely excited. Mum fished in her handbag for her glasses but Julia was already staring at the old yellow newspaper. At the top it said in Gothic capitals '**Darnley-in-Makerfield Examiner**, 27th March, 1888,' and underneath she read the head-line.

Coroner Warns about the Dangers of Reading in Bed

Sir Austen Greenald, Coroner for North West Lancashire, warned yesterday of the dangers of lighted candles in confined spaces. He was presiding at the inquest on Jane Heslop, chambermaid of 19 Baillie Square, Darnley, who had been found dead at the house on 19th February. The court listened to his summing up in which he conjectured that the deceased, described by her employer, Mr Albert Birdsall, as 'a most dutiful and honest girl, and one anxious to extend her education' must have been reading late at night and, exhausted by her day's labours, fallen asleep, letting her lighted candle drop to the ground. Bedding, drapery and matting were all consumed and it is thought that the deceased, overcome by smoke before she could reach door or window, died of suffocation.'

'19th February,' Dad said quietly. 'That was the day we went to the Town Hall.'

'Oh yes,' Aunt Annie said when they showed her the newspaper. 'Poor little Janey Heslop. She was a right marvel she was, my mam told me all about her, up every morning at four, carrying hot water cans, black-leading all the grates, washing them tiles down. No wonder she fell asleep at her books, poor little mite, she were only fourteen. My dad gave her a proper funeral apparently, horses and all. She hadn't got no family. They put her little coffin up on the first landing, so folk could come and pay their respects. There wasn't room in the hall, it's that narrow. Oh aye, my mam told me all about little Janey Heslop. They never let servants sleep in them attics after. Then my father had the gas put in.'

The Bostocks stayed on at Aunt Annie's and Julia got to like living in Baillie Square. She got to like her new friends and her new school. She even got to like the house. They had a deep red carpet laid on the stairs and that awful cold feeling by the rocking-horse never came again. Great-aunt Annie said it was because poor Janey was at peace now, she'd just had to 'stay on for a bit', till Loll was safe. They'd said a little prayer for Janey one night, after his story and his sweet, because she didn't come to see him any more and he missed her.

Six months after the fire Julia got a medal and a special certificate from something called The Royal Humane Society, because she'd been so brave on the night it happened. Loll was a bit jealous, soldiers had medals and this one was very big and shiny.

Still, he'd got his candlestick and that was shiny too now. Mum put it on his bookshelf with all his very special things and when he got frightened in the dark he switched his light on and looked at it for a minute. It reminded him of the lady.

The story of the servant girl who died while reading in bed is true. The original story appeared in the *Oxford Times* a hundred years ago. She lived in St John Street.

The Shadow-Cage

PHILIPPA PEARCE

The little green stoppered bottle had been waiting in the earth a long time for someone to find it. Ned Challis found it. High on his tractor as he ploughed the field, he'd been keeping a look-out, as usual, for whatever might turn up. Several times there had been worked flints; once, one of an enormous size.

Now sunlight glimmering on glass caught his eye. He stopped the tractor, climbed down, picked the bottle from the earth. He could tell at once that it wasn't all that old. Not as old as the flints that he'd taken to the museum in Castleford. Not as old as a coin he had once found, with the head of a Roman emperor on it. Not very old; but old.

Perhaps just useless old . . .

He held the bottle in the palm of his hand and thought of throwing it away. The lip of it was chipped badly, and the stopper of cork or wood had sunk into

the neck. With his finger-nail he tried to move it. The stopper had hardened into stone, and stuck there. Probably no one would ever get it out now without breaking the bottle. But then, why should anyone want to unstopper the bottle? It was empty, or as good as empty. The bottom of the inside of the bottle was dirtied with something blackish and scaly that also clung a little to the sides.

He wanted to throw the bottle away, but he didn't. He held it in one hand while the fingers of the other cleaned the remaining earth from the outside. When he had cleaned it, he didn't fancy the bottle any more than before; but he dropped it into his pocket. Then he climbed the tractor and started off again.

At that time the sun was high in the sky, and the tractor was working on Whistlers' Hill, which is part of Belper's Farm, fifty yards below Burnt House. As the tractor moved on again, the gulls followed again, rising and falling in their flights, wheeling over the disturbed earth, looking for live things, for food; for good things.

That evening, at tea, Ned Challis brought the bottle out and set it on the table by the loaf of bread. His wife looked at it suspiciously: 'Another of your dirty old things for that museum?'

Ned said: 'It's not museum-stuff. Lisa can have it to take to school. I don't want it.'

Mrs Challis pursed her lips, moved the loaf further away from the bottle, and went to refill the teapot.

Lisa took the bottle in her hand. 'Where'd you get it, Dad?'

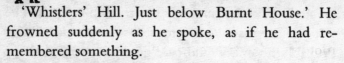

'Whistlers' Hill. Just below Burnt House.' He frowned suddenly as he spoke, as if he had remembered something.

'What's it got inside?'

'Nothing. And if you try getting the stopper out, that'll break.'

So Lisa didn't try. Next morning she took it to school; but she didn't show it to anyone. Only her cousin Kevin saw it, and that was before school and by accident. He always called for Lisa on his way to school – there was no other company on that country road – and he saw her pick up the bottle from the table, where her mother had left it the night before, and put it into her anorak pocket.

'What was that?' asked Kevin.

'You saw. A little old bottle.'

'Let's see it again – properly.' Kevin was younger than Lisa and she sometimes indulged him; so she took the bottle out and let him hold it.

At once he tried the stopper.

'Don't,' said Lisa. 'You'll only break it.'

'What's inside?'

'Nothing. Dad found it on Whistlers'.'

'It's not very nice, is it?'

'What do you mean, "Not very nice"?'

'I don't know. But let me keep it for a bit. Please, Lisa.'

On principle Lisa now decided not to give in. 'Certainly not. Give it back.'

He did, reluctantly. 'Let me have it just for today, at school. Please.'

'No.'

'I'll give you something if you'll let me have it. I'll not let anyone else touch it; I'll not let them see it. I'll keep it safe. Just for today.'

'You'd only break it. No. What could you give me, anyway?'

'My week's pocket-money.'

'No. I've said no and I mean no, young Kev.'

'I'd give you that little china dog you like.'

'The one with the china kennel?'

'Yes.'

'The china dog with the china kennel – you'd give me both?'

'Yes.'

'Only for half the day, then,' said Lisa. 'I'll let you have it after school-dinner – look out for me in the playground. Give it back at the end of school. Without fail. And you be careful with it.'

So the bottle travelled to school in Lisa's anorak pocket, where it bided its time all morning. After school-dinner Lisa met Kevin in the playground and they withdrew together to a corner which was well away from the crowded climbing-frame and the infants' sand-pit and the rest. Lisa handed the bottle over. 'At the end of school, mind, without fail. And if we miss each other then,' – for Lisa, being in a higher class, came out of school slightly later than Kevin – 'then you must drop it in at ours as you pass. Promise.'

'Promise.'

They parted. Kevin put the bottle into his pocket. He didn't know why he'd wanted the bottle, but he had. Lots of things were like that. You needed them for a bit; and then you didn't need them any longer.

He had needed this little bottle very much.

He left Lisa and went over to the climbing-frame, where his friends already were. He had set his foot on a rung when he thought suddenly how easy it would be for the glass bottle in his trouser pocket to be smashed against the metal framework. He stepped down again and went over to the fence that separated the playground from the farmland beyond. Tall tussocks of grass grew along it, coming through from the open fields and fringing the very edge of the asphalt. He looked round: Lisa had already gone in, and no one else was watching. He put his hand into his pocket and took it out again with the bottle concealed in the fist. He stooped as if to examine an insect on a tussock, and slipped his hand into the middle of it and left the bottle there, well hidden.

He straightened up and glanced around. Since no one was looking in his direction, his action had been unobserved; the bottle would be safe. He ran back to the climbing-frame and began to climb, jostling and shouting and laughing, as he and his friends always did. He forgot the bottle.

He forgot the bottle completely.

It was very odd, considering what a fuss he had made about the bottle, that he should have forgotten it; but he did. When the bell rang for the end of playtime, he ran straight in. He did not think of the bottle then, or later. At the end of afternoon school, he did not remember it; and he happened not to see Lisa, who would surely have reminded him.

Only when he was nearly home, and passing the Challises' house, he remembered. He had faithfully promised – and had really meant to keep his promise. But he'd broken it, and left the bottle behind. If he turned and went back to school now, he would meet Lisa, and she would have to be told . . . By the time he got back to the school playground, all his friends would have gone home: the caretaker would be there, and perhaps a late teacher or two, and they'd all want to know what he was up to. And when he'd got the bottle and dropped it in at the Challises', Lisa would scold him all over again. And when he got home at last, he would be very late for his tea, and his mother would be angry.

As he stood by the Challises' gate, thinking, it seemed best, since he had messed things up anyway, to go straight home and leave the bottle to the next day. So he went home.

He worried about the bottle for the rest of the day, without having the time or the quiet to think about it very clearly. He knew that Lisa would assume he had just forgotten to leave it at her house on the way home. He half expected her to turn up after tea, to claim it; but she didn't. She would have been angry enough about his having forgotten to leave it; but what about her anger tomorrow on the way to school, when she found that he had forgotten it altogether – abandoned it in the open playground? He thought of hurrying straight past her house in the morning; but he would never manage it. She would be on the look-out.

He saw that he had made the wrong decision earlier. He ought, at all costs, to have gone back to the play-ground to get the bottle.

He went to bed, still worrying. He fell asleep, and his worry went on, making his dreaming unpleasant in a nagging way. He must be quick, his dreams seemed to nag. *Be quick* . . .

Suddenly he was wide awake. It was very late. The sound of the television being switched off must have woken him. Quietness. He listened to the rest of the family going to bed. They went to bed and to sleep. Silence. They were all asleep now, except for him. He couldn't sleep.

Then, as abruptly as if someone had lifted the top of his head like a lid and popped the idea in, he saw that this time – almost the middle of the night – was the perfect time for him to fetch the bottle. He knew by heart the roads between home and school; he would not be afraid. He would have plenty of time. When he reached the school, the gate to the play-ground would be shut, but it was not high: in the past, by daylight, he and his friends had often climbed it. He would go into the playground, find the correct tussock of grass, get the bottle, bring it back, and have it ready to give to Lisa on the way to school in the morning. She would be angry, but only moderately angry. She would never know the whole truth.

He got up and dressed quickly and quietly. He began to look for a pocket torch, but gave up when he realized that would mean opening and shutting drawers and cupboards. Anyway, there was a moon tonight, and he knew his way, and he knew the school playground. He couldn't go wrong.

He let himself out of the house, leaving the door on the latch for his return. He looked at his watch: between a quarter and half past eleven – not as late as he had thought. All the same, he set off almost at a run, but had to settle down into a steady trot. His trotting footsteps on the road sounded clearly in the night quiet. But who was there to hear?

He neared the Challises' house. He drew level with it.

Ned Challis heard. Usually nothing woke him before the alarm clock in the morning; but tonight footsteps woke him. Who, at this hour – he lifted the back of his wrist towards his face, so that the time glimmered at him – who, at nearly twenty-five to twelve, could be hurrying along that road on foot? When the footsteps had almost gone – when it was already perhaps too late – he sprang out of bed and over to the window.

His wife woke. 'What's up, then, Ned?'

'Just somebody. I wondered who.'

'Oh, come back to bed!'

Ned Challis went back to bed; but almost at once got out again.

'Ned! What is it now?'

'I just thought I'd have a look at Lisa.'

At once Mrs Challis was wide awake. 'What's wrong with Lisa?'

'Nothing.' He went to listen at Lisa's door – listen to the regular, healthy breathing of her sleep. He came back. 'Nothing. Lisa's all right.'

'For Heaven's sake! Why shouldn't she be?'

'Well, who was it walking out there? Hurrying.'

'Oh, go to sleep!'

'Yes.' He lay down again, drew the bedclothes round him, lay still. But his eyes remained open.

Out in the night, Kevin left the road on which the Challises lived and came into the more important one that would take him into the village. He heard the rumble of a lorry coming up behind him. For safety he drew right into a gateway and waited. The lorry came past at a steady pace, headlights on. For a few seconds he saw the driver and his mate sitting up in the cab, intent on the road ahead. He had not wanted to be noticed by them, but, when they had gone, he felt lonely.

He went on into the village, its houses lightless, its streets deserted. By the entrance to the school driveway, he stopped to make sure he was unobserved. Nobody. Nothing – not even a cat. There was no sound of any vehicle now; but in the distance he heard a dog barking, and then another answered it. A little owl cried and cried for company or for sport. Then that, too, stopped.

He turned into the driveway to the school, and there was the gate to the playground. He looked over it, into the playground. Moonlight showed him everything: the expanse of asphalt, the sand-pit, the big climbing-frame, and – at the far end – the fence with the tussocks of grass growing blackly along it. It was all familiar, and yet strange because of the emptiness and the whitening of moonlight and the shadows cast like solid things. The climbing-frame reared high into the air, and on the ground stretched the black criss-cross of its shadows like the bars of a cage.

But he had not come all this way to be halted by moonshine and insubstantial shadows. In a business-like way he climbed the gate and crossed the playground to the fence. He wondered whether he would find the right tussock easily, but he did. His fingers closed on the bottle: it was waiting for him.

At that moment, in the Challises' house, as they lay side by side in bed, Mrs Challis said to her husband: 'You're still awake, aren't you?'

'Yes.'

'What is it?'

'Nothing.'

Mrs Challis sighed.

'All right, then,' said Ned Challis. 'It's this. That bottle I gave Lisa – that little old bottle that I gave Lisa yesterday –'

'What about it?'

'I found it by Burnt House.'

145

Mrs Challis drew in her breath sharply. Then she said, 'That may mean nothing.' Then, 'How near was it?'

'Near enough.' After a pause: 'I ought never to have given it to Lisa. I never thought. But Lisa's all right, anyway.'

'But, Ned, don't you know what Lisa did with that bottle?'

'What?'

'Lent it to Kevin to have at school. And, according to her, he didn't return it when he should have done, on the way home. Didn't you hear her going on and on about it?'

'Kevin . . .' For the third time that night Ned Challis was getting out of bed, this time putting on his trousers, fumbling for his shoes. 'Somebody went up the road in a hurry. You know – I looked out. I couldn't see properly, but it was somebody small. It could have been a child. It could have been Lisa, but it wasn't. It could well have been Kevin . . .'

'Shouldn't you go to their house first, Ned – find out whether Kevin is there or not? Make sure. You're not sure.'

'I'm not sure. But, if I wait to make sure, I may be too late.'

Mrs Challis did not say, 'Too late for what?' She did not argue.

Ned Challis dressed and went down. As he let himself out of the house to get his bicycle from the shed, the church clock began to strike the hour, the sound reaching him distantly across the intervening fields. He checked with his watch: midnight.

In the village, in the school playground, the striking of midnight sounded clangorously close. Kevin stood with the bottle held in the palm of his hand, waiting for the clock to stop striking – waiting as if for something to follow.

After the last stroke of midnight, there was silence, but Kevin stood still waiting and listening. A car or lorry passed the entrance of the school drive: he heard it distinctly; yet it was oddly faint, too. He couldn't place the oddness of it. It had sounded much further away than it should have done – less really there.

He gripped the bottle and went on listening, as if for some particular sound. The minutes passed. The same dog barked at the same dog, bark and reply – far, unreally far away. The little owl called; from another world, it might have been.

He was gripping the bottle so tightly now that his hand was sweating. He felt his skin begin to prickle with sweat at the back of his neck and under his arms.

Then there was a whistle from across the fields, distantly. It should have been an unexpected sound, just after midnight; but it did not startle him. It did set him off across the playground, however. Too late he wanted to get away. He had to go past the climbing-frame, whose cagework of shadows now stretched more largely than the frame itself. He saw the bars of shadow as he approached; he actually hesitated; and then, like a fool, he stepped inside the cage of shadows.

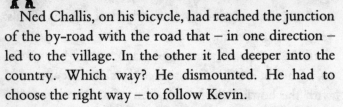

Ned Challis, on his bicycle, had reached the junction of the by-road with the road that – in one direction – led to the village. In the other it led deeper into the country. Which way? He dismounted. He had to choose the right way – to follow Kevin.

Thinking of Whistlers' Hill, he turned the front wheel of his bicycle away from the village and set off again. But now, with his back to the village, going away from the village, he felt a kind of weariness and despair. A memory of childhood came into his mind: a game he had played in childhood: something hidden for him to find, and if he turned in the wrong direction to search, all the voices whispered to him, 'Cold – cold!' Now, with the village receding behind him, he recognized what he felt: cold . . . cold . . .

Without getting off his bicycle, he wheeled round and began to pedal hard in the direction of the village.

In the playground, there was no pressing hurry for Kevin any more. He did not press against the bars of his cage to get out. Even when clouds cut off the moonlight and the shadows melted into general darkness – even when the shadow-cage was no longer visible to the eye, he stood there; then crouched there, in a corner of the cage, as befitted a prisoner.

The church clock struck the quarter.

The whistlers were in no hurry. The first whistle had come from right across the fields. Then there was a long pause. Then the sound was repeated, equally distantly, from the direction of the river bridges. Later still, another whistle from the direction of the railway line, or somewhere near it.

He lay in his cage, cramped by the bars, listening. He did not know he was thinking, but suddenly it came to him: Whistlers' Hill. He and Lisa and the others had always supposed that the hill had belonged to a family called Whistler, as Challises' house belonged to the Challis family. But that was not how the hill had got its name – he saw that now. No, indeed not.

Whistler answered whistler at long intervals, like the sentries of a besieging army. There was no moving in as yet.

The church clock had struck the quarter as Ned Challis entered the village and cycled past the entrance to the school. He cycled as far as the Recreation Ground, perhaps because that was where Kevin would have gone in the daytime. He cycled bumpily round the Ground: no Kevin.

He began to cycle back the way he had come, as though he had given up altogether and were going home. He cycled slowly. He passed the entrance to the school again.

In this direction, he was leaving the village. He was cycling so slowly that the front wheel of his bicycle wobbled desperately; the light from his dynamo was dim. He put a foot down and stopped. Motionless, he listened. There was nothing to hear, unless – yes, the faintest ghost of a sound, high pitched, prolonged for seconds, remote as from another world. Like a coward

– and Ned Challis was no coward – he tried to persuade himself that he had imagined the sound; yet he knew he had not. It came from another direction now: very faint, yet penetrating, so that his skin crinkled to hear it. Again it came, from yet another quarter.

He wheeled his bicycle back to the entrance to the school and left it there. He knew he must be very close. He walked up to the playground gate and peered over it. But the moon was obscured by cloud: he could see nothing. He listened, waited for the moon to sail free.

In the playground Kevin had managed to get up, first on his hands and knees, then upright. He was very much afraid, but he had to be standing to meet whatever it was.

For the whistlers had begun to close in slowly, surely: converging on the school, on the school playground, on the cage of shadows. On him.

For some time now cloud-masses had obscured the moon. He could see nothing; but he felt the whistlers' presence. Their signals came more often, and always closer. Closer. Very close.

Suddenly the moon sailed free.

In the sudden moonlight Ned Challis saw clear across the playground to where Kevin stood against the climbing-frame, with his hands writhing together in front of him.

In the sudden moonlight Kevin did not see his uncle. Between him and the playground gate, and all round him, air was thickening into darkness. Frantically he tried to undo his fingers, that held the little bottle, so that he could throw it from him. But he could not. He held the bottle; the bottle held him.

The darkness was closing in on him. The darkness was about to take him; had surely got him.

Kevin shrieked.

Ned Challis shouted: 'I'm here!' and was over the gate and across the playground and with his arms round the boy: '*I've got you.*'

There was a tinkle as something fell from between Kevin's opened fingers: the little bottle fell and rolled to the middle of the playground. It lay there, very insignificant-looking.

Kevin was whimpering and shaking, but he could move of his own accord. Ned Challis helped him over the gate and to the bicycle.

'Do you think you could sit on the bar, Kev? Could you manage that?'

'Yes.' He could barely speak.

Ned Challis hesitated, thinking of the bottle which had chosen to come to rest in the very centre of the playground, where the first child tomorrow would see it, pick it up.

He went back and picked the bottle up. Wherever he threw it, someone might find it. He might smash it and grind the pieces underfoot; but he was not sure he dared to do that.

Anyway, he was not going to hold it in his hand longer than he strictly must. He put it into his pocket, and then, when he got back to Kevin and the bicycle, he slipped it into the saddle-bag.

He rode Kevin home on the crossbar of his bicycle. At the Challises' front gate Mrs Challis was waiting, with the dog for company. She just said: 'He all right then?'

'Ah.'

'I'll make a cup of tea while you take him home.'

At his own front door, Kevin said: 'I left the door on the latch. I can get in. I'm all right. I'd rather – I'd rather –'

'Less spoken of, the better,' said his uncle. 'You go to bed. Nothing to be afraid of now.'

He waited until Kevin was inside the house and he heard the latch click into place. Then he rode back to his wife, his cup of tea, and consideration of the problem that lay in his saddle-bag.

After he had told his wife everything, and they had discussed possibilities, Ned Challis said thoughtfully: 'I might take it to the museum, after all. Safest place for it would be inside a glass case there.'

'But you said they wouldn't want it.'

'Perhaps they would, if I told them where I found it and a bit – only a bit – about Burnt House . . .'

'You do that, then.'

Ned Challis stood up and yawned with a finality that said, Bed.

'But don't you go thinking you've solved all your problems by taking that bottle to Castleford, Ned. Not by a long chalk.'

'No?'

'Lisa. She reckons she owns that bottle.'

'I'll deal with Lisa tomorrow.'

'Today, by the clock.'

Ned Challis gave a groan that turned into another yawn. 'Bed first,' he said; 'then Lisa.' They went to bed not long before the dawn.

The next day and for days after that, Lisa was furiously angry with her father. He had as good as stolen her bottle, she said, and now he refused to give it back, to let her see it, even to tell her what he had done with it. She was less angry with Kevin. (She did not know, of course, the circumstances of the bottle's passing from Kevin to her father.)

Kevin kept out of Lisa's way, and even more carefully kept out of his uncle's. He wanted no private conversation.

One Saturday Kevin was having tea at the Challises', because he had been particularly invited. He sat with Lisa and Mrs Challis. Ned had gone to Castleford, and came in late. He joined them at the tea-table in evident good spirits. From his pocket he brought out a small cardboard box, which he placed in the centre of the table, by the Saturday cake. His wife was staring at him: before he spoke, he gave her the slightest nod of reassurance. 'The museum didn't want to keep that little old glass bottle, after all,' he said.

Both the children gave a cry: Kevin started up with such a violent backward movement that his chair clattered to the floor behind him; Lisa leant forward, her fingers clawing towards the box.

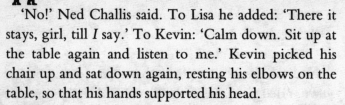

'No!' Ned Challis said. To Lisa he added: 'There it stays, girl, till *I* say.' To Kevin: 'Calm down. Sit up at the table again and listen to me.' Kevin picked his chair up and sat down again, resting his elbows on the table, so that his hands supported his head.

'Now,' said Ned Challis, 'you two know so much that it's probably better you should know more. That little old bottle came from Whistlers' Hill, below Burnt House – well, you know that. Burnt House is only a ruin now – elder bushes growing inside as well as out; but once it was a cottage that someone lived in. Your mother's granny remembered the last one to live there.'

'No, Ned,' said Mrs Challis, 'it was my great-granny remembered.'

'Anyway,' said Ned Challis, 'it was so long ago that Victoria was the Queen, that's certain. And an old woman lived alone in that cottage. There were stories about her.'

'Was she a witch?' breathed Lisa.

'So they said. They said she went out on the hillside at night –'

'At the full of the moon,' said Mrs Challis.

'They said she dug up roots and searched out plants and toadstools and things. They said she caught rats and toads and even bats. They said she made ointments and powders and weird brews. And they said she used what she made to cast spells and call up spirits.'

'Spirits from Hell, my great-granny said. Real bad 'uns.'

'So people said, in the village. Only the parson

scoffed at the whole idea. Said he'd called often and
been shown over the cottage and seen nothing out of
the ordinary – none of the jars and bottles of stuff that
she was supposed to have for her witchcraft. He said
she was just a poor cranky old woman; that was all.

'Well, she grew older and older and crankier and
crankier, and one day she died. Her body lay in its
coffin in the cottage, and the parson was going to
bury her next day in the churchyard.

'The night before she was to have been buried,
someone went up from the village –'

'Someone!' said Mrs Challis scornfully. 'Tell them
the whole truth, Ned, if you're telling the story at all.
Half the village went up, with lanterns – men, women,
and children. Go on, Ned.'

'The cottage was thatched, and they began to pull
swatches of straw away and take it into the cottage
and strew it round and heap it up under the coffin.
They were going to fire it all.

'They were pulling the straw on the downhill side
of the cottage when suddenly a great piece of thatch
came away and out came tumbling a whole lot of
things that the old woman must have kept hidden
there. People did hide things in thatches, in those days.'

'Her savings?' asked Lisa.

'No. A lot of jars and little bottles, all stoppered or
sealed, neat and nice. With stuff inside.'

There was a silence at the tea-table. Then Lisa said:
'That proved it: she was a witch.'

'Well, no, it only proved she *thought* she was a

witch. That was what the parson said afterwards – and whew! was he mad when he knew about that night.'

Mrs Challis said: 'He gave it 'em red-hot from the pulpit the next Sunday. He said that once upon a time poor old deluded creatures like her had been burnt alive for no reason at all, and the village ought to be ashamed of having burnt her dead.'

Lisa went back to the story of the night itself. 'What did they do with what came out of the thatch?'

'Bundled it inside the cottage among the straw, and fired it all. The cottage burnt like a beacon that night, they say. Before cock-crow, everything had been burnt to ashes. That's the end of the story.'

'Except for my little bottle,' said Lisa. 'That came out of the thatch, but it didn't get picked up. It rolled downhill, or someone kicked it.'

'That's about it,' Ned agreed.

Lisa stretched her hand again to the cardboard box, and this time he did not prevent her. But he said: 'Don't be surprised, Lisa. It's different.'

She paused. 'A different bottle?'

'The same bottle, but – well, you'll see.'

Lisa opened the box, lifted the packaging of cotton wool, took the bottle out. It was the same bottle, but the stopper had gone, and it was empty and clean – so clean that it shone greenly. Innocence shone from it.

'You said the stopper would never come out,' Lisa said slowly.

'They forced it by suction. The museum chap wanted to know what was inside, so he got the hospital lab to take a look – he has a friend there. It was easy for them.'

Mrs Challis said: 'That would make a pretty vase, Lisa. For tiny flowers.' She coaxed Lisa to go out to pick a posy from the garden; she herself took the bottle away to fill it with water.

Ned Challis and Kevin faced each other across the table.

Kevin said: 'What was in it?'

Ned Challis said: 'A trace of this, a trace of that, the hospital said. One thing more than anything else.'

'Yes?'

'Blood. Human blood.'

Lisa came back with her flowers; Mrs Challis came back with the bottle filled with water. When the flowers had been put in, it looked a pretty thing.

'My witch-bottle,' said Lisa contentedly. 'What was she called – the old woman that thought she was a witch?'

Her father shook his head; her mother thought: 'Madge – or was it Maggy –?'

'Maggy Whistler's bottle, then,' said Lisa.

'Oh, no,' said Mrs Challis. 'She was Maggy – or Madge – Dawson. I remember my granny saying so. Dawson.'

'Then why's it called Whistlers' Hill?'

'I'm not sure,' said Mrs Challis uneasily. 'I mean, I don't think anyone knows for certain.'

But Ned Challis, looking at Kevin's face, knew that he knew for certain.

Spring-heeled Jack

GWEN GRANT

To Anna, the day they moved was the most exciting of her life.

She raced up and down with pictures and pans and
odd things that had been left out of boxes.

At last, it was finished. The flat was empty and the
bare rooms looked slightly tawdry with everything
gone. The rain lashed the wide windows and Anna
closed the door behind her, glad they were leaving.

Her mother fussed about the times of the buses.

'If we get one straight into town, we'll be at the
house in oh, what, fifteen minutes? Yes, fifteen
minutes. Come on, Anna. We'll have to get a move
on.'

They hurried along the desolate street. Because of
the rain, none of Anna's friends were out playing and
her mother had kept her too busy to go round knocking on doors and saying goodbye.

'It isn't as if you're going to the end of the world,'

her mother said. 'You'll probably see them just as often,' but Anna had a feeling she wouldn't.

Despite everything, she could only feel pleased they were moving.

She looked back once. The block of flats sat in its place in the row of blocks. They looked like an unimaginative Stonehenge. High up one concrete wall, she could see their bare windows, blank faced without her mother's net curtains.

By the following week, someone else would be living there but Anna, her mother, father and brother Jason, they would be living in the small terraced house they were now making their way to.

By six o'clock the little house glowed with light and warmth. An enormous coal fire leapt and twisted up the chimney and Anna kept breaking off her work to look at it.

She had never lived where you could have a proper fire before and she found it enchanting.

She'd read about making pictures in the fire and now she could do it for herself. Those pieces of coal at one side, they looked like rocks. Rocks that a determined prince would ride up perhaps, to rescue a damsel in distress. Down the sides of the black lumps, a liquid rope of fire turned into long golden tresses.

Unthinkingly, Anna ran a hand over her own plain brown plaits.

'Come on, Anna. Get a move on,' her mother nudged her impatiently, splintering her day-dream. 'There'll be plenty of time to look in the fire when we've got sorted out a bit more,' and then her eyes fell on the clock. 'Look at the time,' she said in breathless amazement. 'The dog hasn't been for a walk yet and here I am with not a drop of milk in the house.'

She crossed the small untidy room to ferret for her purse on the mantelpiece.

'Look, love,' she said. 'Get Toby and go down to the shop at the bottom of the road and get us a pint of milk. Kill two birds with one stone, that way.'

Anna put her hooded duffle-coat on and tied a blue and white striped scarf round her neck.

'Come on, Tobe,' she called to the nervous dog, who was looking for his vanished basket.

'Poor old Tobe,' she crooned, patting his rough head.

When Toby saw the lead, he forgot about his missing bed and started to jump. Outside lay a whole new world and it was one he couldn't wait to investigate.

Anna opened the old wooden door carefully. She was used to a modern glass door with metal leaves curling their way up the frosted panel, but she liked the old door. It wasn't a very nice colour. Dark green.

'Hospital paint that,' her dad said. 'Probably giving it away. Can't imagine anybody buying that colour, can you, Jean?' he asked his wife and she looked round the dark green kitchen and thought of the dark green lavatory and dark green back bedroom and nodded her head.

'Wherever it came from,' she said. 'I wish it hadn't.'

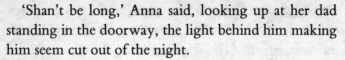

'Shan't be long,' Anna said, looking up at her dad standing in the doorway, the light behind him making him seem cut out of the night.

'And watch your step,' he called. 'Don't talk to no strangers and come straight back.'

'I'll be all right, Dad,' Anna said and she and Toby walked down the street.

At first Anna was so busy looking round her, she found the darkness didn't bother her at all.

Theirs was a shortish street leading on to a much longer street of houses that tumbled down a steep hill. Two houses and a long dark passage. Two houses and a long dark passage. That was how they were set out.

It was only drizzling now and Anna's feet squelched wetly on the shining pavement. Toby hurried along, nose to the ground, somehow managing to pick up an interesting smell every now and again despite the rain.

It was while Anna was walking past one of the passages that she thought she saw a movement out of the corner of her eye. She turned her head sharply but there was no one there. No one that she could see, anyway.

The dark gaping mouth of the passage stared back blindly.

Anna took a deep breath and shook herself sternly.

'You're just frightening yourself for nothing,' she said to Toby in a sharp voice.

Toby looked up, his head on one side.

'There's nothing there, old Tobe, is there?' Anna asked the dog and the dog stared down the passage, curled his top lip back and started to snarl. The snarl turned into a choking wail as he pulled on the lead, his head straining towards the dark hole.

Anna pulled him back, hesitated a second and then took to her heels. She flew down the street, Toby running unwillingly alongside her. She could feel the dog's head turning as he pulled on the lead but she kept running.

In two short minutes, she was standing in the safety of the lighted shop doorway.

Anna leant against the shop window, her breath catching in her throat. Her heart was beating so heavily, it hurt.

After a minute or two, she felt able to go into the shop. The woman behind the counter stared at her but all she saw was a girl with cheeks rosy from running, her hair beaded with silvery speckles of rain where the duffle hood had fallen back from her face.

'Evening,' the woman said and Anna wondered if she should tell her about the passage, but tell her what? She hadn't seen anything. It was only Toby who'd growled and carried on.

She bought the pint of milk and put it in the carrier bag her mother had given her.

When she was out of the shop, she looked up the long dark hilly street and blazed with relief to see her brother walking towards her.

'Dad sent me to meet you,' he grumbled. 'Dunno why. There's not much can happen between here and home.'

'I don't know about that,' Anna said weakly and told Jason about the passageway.

'Probably a cat,' he shrugged. 'You know what Toby is for cats,' and Anna laughed.

Of course, she thought, why hadn't she realized it was probably a cat.

They walked up the street, chattering about the day. About how different these small dark streets were to the wide orange-lit streets of the estate. They walked past lighted windows which were only slightly taller than themselves.

'I really like this,' Toby said. 'You look up and all you see is sky. No windows staring down at you like in the flats.'

'And nobody throwing things at you either,' Anna replied.

They were so engrossed in their talk that the only warning they had was when Toby sprang forward on his lead, barking wildly.

In front of them, near enough to be touched, a giant shadow catapulted out of a passageway. The shadow flew high in the air, came down heavily, bent until it was half its size and then, with another leap, had vanished.

Anna saw a monstrous creature, dark as the night itself, in front of her. It seemed to jump as high as the houses. She felt her cheek grazed by the flick of a hard material. Then the giant became a dwarf whose pale oval face was almost on a level with Anna's. She caught a glimpse of spiteful bright eyes and then the face was gone.

It happened so quickly and so soundlessly that the two children were still gaping at where the apparition had been by the time it had gone. They hadn't even had a chance to move their positions.

And then Anna opened her mouth and screamed and screamed and screamed, while Jason, white faced, tried to comfort her.

The street came alive with noise and people. Lights went on, doors flew open, people fell out of their houses, all exclaiming and asking questions.

'Who?' 'What?' 'Why?' 'Where?' 'When?', they called, shouted and demanded.

They quickly had the story out of the two children but it turned out to be an old story.

'Spring-heeled Jack,' they said angrily and the men got together in a tense crowd.

The police came. The people were sent home. Anna and Jason taken home.

'He doesn't do anything,' the policeman told their parents. 'All he does is jump out and then disappear.'

'He was a giant,' Anna wailed.

'Massive,' Jason agreed. 'But little too,' and Anna thought of those white eyes staring into hers and she shuddered.

The men were going to search the streets. The police were in and out of the passages and back gardens but after a thorough look, they came up empty handed.

'Never find anything,' Anna heard. 'He comes and goes like a blooming ghost.'

'There's nothing ghostly about this graze on my daughter's face,' Anna's mother said tartly.

The days passed. The memory of Spring-heeled Jack lessened a little, her cheek started to heal and Anna went to bed more easily. She started to treat the small streets with caution.

From time to time, they heard of more jumpings. The lodger next door said, 'It's since they pulled down the old Church, I tell you. If you asks me, they let something out of there,' and Anna, looking at him, felt a slight sense of recognition.

Recoiling from the lodger, she dodged behind her father's back.

The lodger's mouth curved in a smile but he never smiled directly at anyone with his eyes. He always smiled at the floor.

Anna's mother glanced sharply at the man but he held his teacup so carefully. He put it on the table so gently. He seemed a grey, careful, gentle man.

Anna asked if anyone had a picture of the old Church and the lodger said he had.

'I'll get it you,' he said and came back with it held tightly in his thick fingers.

The girl studied the picture intently, going back to it again and again.

The lodger smiled as he watched her.

Later that evening when Anna and her mother walked past the waste ground where the Church had once stood, Anna said, 'Do you think the lodger's telling the truth?'

'What?' said her mother. 'About the Church? Lot of nonsense. Ought to have more sense scaring folk half to death. I'll have a word with him,' she finished, angry again as she remembered the lodger's words and saw her daughter's strained face.

Anna stared at the waste ground all the time they were walking past it. The land was dark and deserted. She shivered and turned her head but a flickering point of light drew her attention. She looked away but had to look back. It was still there.

'Mum,' she whispered. 'Look. That light,' and her mother turned and looked.

'Where?' she said.

'There,' Anna pointed.

The light was like Spring-heeled Jack. One minute it seemed large. The next, it almost disappeared.

'My word,' her mother said crossly. 'We'll see about this,' and she moved towards the nearest house. 'We'll get some help, Anna, and go and see exactly what's going on there.'

The people in the house got other people and they all went to see what the light was.

It was just a candle, pressed into the earth, burning. Beside it lay an untidy scattering of grey stone.

'Why it looks like an altar candle,' a man said, leaving the long white candle where it was. 'Steal anything these days they will. Anything that isn't tied down. Steal the breath out of your mouth if they could.'

Anna flinched as she thought of someone stealing the breath from her mouth.

She moved the stones with her foot then turned away.

'I'll wait over here,' she told her mother, and made her way back across the waste land. Back to the street and the lamp-posts.

She had almost reached the pavement when she felt a prickling on her skin.

Sharply, she turned round and there, standing against the dark wall, was a black shadow. The next instant, Spring-heeled Jack lurched towards her and then his familiar movements appeared. Anna saw the dark shape leap up into the air and it seemed as if he had taken her breath after all, because when Anna tried to scream, no sound came out of her open mouth.

By the candle, someone glanced over.

'It's him,' they shouted, 'It's him,' and a stream of people poured across the rough uneven land.

They put Anna to bed with a glass of hot milk and a tablet from the Doctor.

'They didn't catch him, did they?' she asked harshly.

Her mother shook her head.

'He's after me,' Anna cried. 'Why? What does he want? Why is he picking on me?'

Her parents looked helplessly at each other. The move was going wrong.

'We should have stayed where we were,' her mother said and locked the doors and drew the curtains. 'Nothing like this ever happened in the flats.'

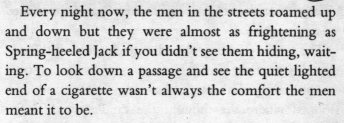

Every night now, the men in the streets roamed up and down but they were almost as frightening as Spring-heeled Jack if you didn't see them hiding, waiting. To look down a passage and see the quiet lighted end of a cigarette wasn't always the comfort the men meant it to be.

The lodger appeared at the back door to ask 'How's the child today?'

Anna's mother retorted sharply, 'Very well. Very well,' and the lodger's plasticine grey face folded itself about with satisfaction.

Anna was sat in a chair, well wrapped up against the cold and the chill of fear that was in her body. She had slept and now she woke as the lodger's voice broke through her sleep.

She turned her eyes on him and followed the curved-down smile. The sense of recognition overwhelmed her tantalizingly.

As if feeling her gaze, the lodger looked straight at her and his malicious flickering eyes stared briefly into hers.

'Still using the picture of the old Church, are you?' he asked, his voice sounding as ancient and rusty as an old key in a lock.

Anna nodded.

The lodger murmured softly and was gone.

Anna reached for the picture and concentrated her attention upon it. Thoughtfully, she traced the printed stonework with her finger. Suddenly, an almost hidden detail leapt out at her. Her breath caught in her throat and she let the picture fall to her knee.

Later that day, Anna made her pilgrimage to the waste ground.

The thin winter sun played at shadows with the ivy climbing over the rubble.

Anna walked through the old Church land and stopped where she thought the candle would have been. She knelt down and moved the debris around with her fingertips, carefully, carefully.

She went in a wider and wider circle and then, pulling back the straggling stems of a clump of weeds, she found what she was looking for.

She picked it up and held it in her hands. The malicious stone face smiled back at her. A gargoyle displaced.

Anna stared sombrely at the grotesque head. She took it down to the old Priory in the town and left it on the font, close to a source of the water that was its life's blood, and where it was sure to be found.

In her mind, she could hear the lodger.

'It's since they pulled down the old Church. They let something out of there.'

Well, Anna thought, brushing the grey dust off her hands. Now they've got it back.

And maybe they had.

Anyway, no one ever heard of Spring-heeled Jack again.

The Spring

PETER DICKINSON

When Derek was seven Great-Aunt Tessa had died and there'd been a funeral party for all the relations. In the middle of it a woman with a face like a sick fish, some kind of cousin, had grabbed hold of Derek and half-talked to him and half-talked to another cousin over his head.

'That's a handsome young fellow, aren't you? (Just like poor old Charlie, that age.) So you're young Derek. How old would you be now, then? (The girls – that's one of them, there, in the green blouse – they're a lot bigger.) Bit of an afterthought, weren't you, Derek? Nice surprise for your mum and dad. (Meg had been meaning to go back to that job of hers, you know . . .)'

And so on, just as if she'd been talking two languages, one he could understand and one he couldn't. Derek hadn't been surprised or shocked. In his heart he'd known all along.

It wasn't that anyone was unkind to him, or even uncaring. Of course his sisters sometimes called him a pest and told him to go away, but mostly the family included him in whatever they were doing and sometimes, not just on his birthday, did something they thought would amuse him. But even those times Derek knew in his heart that he wasn't really meant to be there. If he'd never been born – well, like the cousin said, Mum would have gone back to her job full-time, and five years earlier too, and she'd probably have got promoted so there'd have been more money for things. And better holidays, sooner. And more room in the house – Cindy was always whining about having to share with Fran ... It's funny to think about a world in which you've never existed, never been born. It would seem almost exactly the same to everyone else. They wouldn't miss you – there'd never have been anything for them to miss.

About four years after Great-Aunt Tessa's funeral Dad got a new job and the family moved south. That June Dad and Mum took Derek off to look at a lot of roses. They had their new garden to fill, and there was this famous collection of roses only nine miles away at Something Abbey, so they could go and see if there were ones they specially liked, and get their order in for next winter. Mum and Dad were nuts about gardens. The girls had ploys of their own but it was a tagging-along afternoon for Derek.

The roses grew in a big walled garden, hundreds

and hundreds of them, all different, with labels. Mum and Dad stood in front of each bush in turn, cocking their heads and pursing their lips while they decided if they liked it. They'd smell a bloom or two, and then Mum would read the label and Dad would look it up in his book to see if it was disease-resistant; last of all, Mum might write its name in her notebook and they'd give it marks, out of six, like skating judges, and move on. It took *hours*.

After a bit Mum remembered about Derek.

'Why don't you go down to the house and look at the river, darling? Don't fall in.'

'Got your watch?' said Dad. 'OK, back at the car-park, four-fifteen, sharp.'

He gave Derek 50p in case there were ice-creams anywhere and turned back to the roses.

The river was better than the roses, a bit. The lawn of the big house ran down and became its bank. It was as wide as a road, not very deep but clear, with dark green weed streaming in the current and trout sometimes darting between. Derek found a twig and chucked it in, pacing beside it and timing its speed on his watch. He counted trout for a while, and then walking further along the river he came to a strange shallow stream which ran through the lawns, like a winding path, only water, just a few inches deep but rushing through its channel in quick ripples. Following it up he came to a sort of hole in the ground, with a fence round it. The hole had stone sides and was full of water. The water came rushing up from somewhere underground, almost as though it were boiling. It was very clear. You could see a long way down.

While Derek stood staring, a group of other visitors strolled up and one of them started reading from her guide book, gabbling and missing bits out.

'. . . remarkable spring . . . predates all the rest of the abbey . . . no doubt why the monks settled here . . . white chalk bowl fifteen feet across and twelve feet deep . . . crystal clear water surges out at about two hundred gallons a minute . . . always the same temperature, summer and winter . . .'

'Magical, don't you think?' said another of the tourists.

She didn't mean it. 'Magical' was just a word to her. But yes, Derek thought, magical. Where does it come from? So close to the river, too, but it's got nothing to do with that. Perhaps it comes from another world.

He thought he'd only stood gazing for a short time, hypnotized by the rush of water welling and welling out of nowhere, but when he looked at his watch, it was ten past four. There was an ice-cream van, but Dad and Mum didn't get back to the car till almost twenty to five.

That night Derek dreamed about the spring. Nothing much happened in the dream, only he was standing beside it, looking down. It was night time, with a full moon, and he was waiting for the moon to be reflected from the rumpled water. Something would happen then. He woke before it happened, with his heart hammering. He was filled with a sort of dread, though the dream hadn't been a nightmare. The dread was sort of neutral, half-way between terror and glorious excitement.

The same dream happened the next night, and the next, and the next. When it woke him on the fifth night, he thought: this is getting to be a nuisance.

He got out of bed and went to the window. It was a brilliant night, with a full moon high. He felt wide awake. He turned from the window, meaning to get back into bed, but somehow found himself moving into his getting-up routine, taking his pyjamas off and pulling on his shirt. The moment he realized what he was doing he stopped himself, but then thought why not? It'd fix that dream, at least. He laughed silently to himself and finished dressing. Ten minutes later he was bicycling through the dark.

Derek knew the way to the abbey because Mum was no use at map-reading so that was something he did on car journeys – a way of joining in. He thought he could do it in an hour and a quarter, so he'd be there a bit after one. He'd be pretty tired by the time he got back, but the roads were flat down here compared with Yorkshire. He'd left a note on the kitchen table saying 'Gone for a ride. Back for breakfast.' They'd think he'd just gone out for an early-morning spin – he was always first up. Nine miles there and nine back made eighteen. He'd done fifteen in one go last month. Shouldn't be too bad.

And in fact, although the night was still, he rode as

though there was a stiff breeze at his back, hardly getting tired at all. Late cars swished through the dark. He tried to think of a story in case anyone stopped and asked what he was doing – if a police car came by, it certainly would – but no one did. He reached the abbey at ten past one. The gate was shut, of course. He hadn't even thought about getting in. There might be ivy, or something.

He found some a bit back along the way he'd come, but it wasn't strong or thick enough to climb. Still, it didn't cross his mind he wouldn't get in. He was going to. There would be a way.

The wall turned away from the road beside the garden of another house. Derek wheeled his bike through the gate and pushed it in among some bushes, then followed the wall back through the garden. No light shone from the house. Nobody stirred. He followed the wall of the abbey grounds along towards the back of the garden. He thought he could hear the river rustling beyond. The moonlight was very bright, casting shadows so black they looked solid. The garden became an orchard, heavy old trees, their leafy branches blotting out the moon, but with a clear space further on. Ducking beneath the branches he headed towards it. The night air smelt of something new, sweetish, familiar – fresh-cut sawdust. When he reached the clear space, he found it surrounded a tree-trunk which had had all its branches cut off and just stood there like a twisted arm sticking out of the ground. Leaning against it was a ladder.

It wasn't very heavy. Derek carried it over to the abbey wall. It reached almost to the top. He climbed, straddled the wall, leaned down, and with an effort hauled the ladder up and lowered it on the further side, down into the darkness under the trees that grew there, then climbed down and groped his way out towards where the moonlight gleamed between the tree-trunks. Out in the open on the upper slope of lawn he got his bearings, checked for a landmark so that he would be able to find his way back to the ladder, and walked down in the shadow of the trees towards the river. His heart was beginning to thump, the way it did in the dream. The same dread, between terror and glory, seemed to bubble up inside him.

When he was level with the spring he walked across the open and stood by the low fence, gazing down at the troubled water. It looked very black, and in this light he couldn't see into it at all. He tried to find the exact place he had stood in the dream, and waited. A narrow rim of moon-shadow cast by the wall on the left side edged the disc of water below. It thinned and thinned as the slow-moving moon heeled west. And now it was gone.

The reflection of the moon, broken and scattered by the endlessly upswelling water, began to pass glimmeringly across the disc below. Derek could feel the turn of the world making it move like that. His heartbeat came in hard pulses, seeming to shake his body. Without knowing what he was doing, he climbed the fence and clung to its inner side so that he could gaze straight down into the water. His own reflection, broken by the ripples, was a squat black shape against the silver moonlight. He crouched with his left arm clutching the lowest rail and with his right arm strained down towards it. He could just reach. The black shape changed as the reflection of his arm came to meet it. The water was only water to his touch.

Somehow he found another three inches of stretch and plunged his hand through the surface. The water was still water, but then another hand gripped his.

He almost lost his balance and fell, but the other hand didn't try to pull him in. It didn't let go either. When Derek tried to pull free the hand came with him, and an arm behind it. He pulled, heaved, strained. A head broke the surface. Another arm reached up and gripped the top of the side wall. Now Derek could straighten and take a fresh hold higher up the fence. And now the stranger could climb out, gasping and panting, over the fence and stand on the moonlit lawn beside him. He was a boy about Derek's own age, wearing ordinary clothes like Derek's. They were dry to the touch.

'I thought you weren't coming,' said the boy. 'Have we got somewhere to live?'

'I suppose you'd better come home.'

They walked together towards the trees.

'Who . . .?' began Derek.

'Not now,' said the stranger.

They stole on in silence. We'll have to walk the whole way home, thought Derek. Mightn't get in before breakfast. How'm I going to explain?

The ladder was still against the wall. They climbed it, straddled the top, lowered the ladder the far side and climbed down, propping it back against its tree. Then back towards the road.

There were two bikes hidden in the bushes.

'How on . . .?' began Derek.

'Not now,' said the stranger.

They biked in silence the whole way home, getting in just as the sky was turning grey. They took off their shoes and tiptoed up the stairs. Derek was so tired he couldn't remember going to bed.

They were woken by Cindy's call outside the door.

'Hi! Pests! Get up! School bus in twenty mins!'

Derek scrambled into his clothes and just beat David down the stairs. Dad was in the hallway, looking through the post before driving off to work.

'Morning, twins,' he said. 'Decided to have a lie-in?'

They gobbled their breakfast and caught the bus by running. Jimmy Grove had kept two seats for them. He always did.

Very occasionally during that year Derek felt strange. There was something not quite right in the world, something out of balance, some shadow. It was like that feeling you have when you think you've glimpsed something out of the corner of your eye but when you turn your head it isn't there. Once or twice it was so strong he almost said something. One evening, for instance, he and David were sitting either side of Mum while she leafed through an old photograph album. They laughed or groaned at pictures of themselves as babies, or in fancy dress – Tweedledum and Tweedledee – and then Mum pointed at a picture of an old woman with a crooked grinning face, like a jolly witch, and said, 'I don't suppose you remember her. That's Great-Aunt Tessa. You went to her funeral.'

'I remember the funeral,' said David. 'There was a grisly sort of cousin who grabbed us and told us how handsome we were, and then talked over our heads about us to someone else as if we couldn't understand what she was saying.'

'She had a face like a sick fish,' said Derek.

'Oh, Cousin Vi. She's a pain in the neck. She . . .'

And Mum rattled on about Cousin Vi's murky doings for a bit and then turned the page, but for a moment Derek felt that he had almost grasped the missing what-ever-it-was, almost turned his head quick enough to see something before it vanished. No

On the whole it was a pretty good year. There were dud bits. David broke a leg in the Christmas hols, which spoilt things for a while. The girls kept complaining that the house wasn't big enough for seven, especially with the pests growing so fast, but then Jackie got a job and went to live with friends in a flat in Totton. Dad bought a new car. Those were the most exciting things that happened, so it was a nothing-much year, but not bad. And then one week-end in June Mum and Dad went off to the abbey to look at the roses again. Cindy and Fran were seeing friends, so it was just the twins who tagged along.

The roses were the same as last year, and Mum and Dad slower than ever, so after a bit David said, 'Let's go and look at the river. OK, Mum?'

Dad gave them a quid for ices and told them when to be back at the car. They raced twigs on the river, tried to spot the largest trout, and then found the stream that ran through the lawn and followed it up to the spring. They stood staring at the uprushing water for a long while, not saying anything. In the end Derek looked at his watch, saw it was almost four, woke David from his trance and raced him off to look for ices.

A few nights later Derek woke with his heart pounding. It was something he'd dreamt, but he couldn't remember the dream. He sat up and saw that David's bed was empty. When he got up and put his hand between the sheets, they were still just warm to the touch.

All at once memory came back, the eleven years when he'd been on his own and the year when he'd had David. The other years, the ones when he'd been growing up with a twin brother and the photographs in the album had been taken – they weren't real. By morning he wouldn't remember them. By morning he wouldn't remember David either. There was just this one night.

He rushed into his clothes, crept down the stairs and out. The door was unlocked. David's bike was already gone from the shed. He got his own out and started off.

The night was still, but he felt as though he had an intangible wind in his face. Every pedal-stroke was an effort. He put his head down and rode on. Normally, he knew, he'd be faster than David, whose leg still wasn't properly strong after his accident, but tonight he guessed David would have the spirit wind behind him, the wind from some other world. Derek didn't think he would catch him. All he knew was that he had to try.

In fact he almost ran into him, about two miles from the abbey, just after the turn off the main road. David was trotting along beside his bike, pushing it, gasping for breath.

'What's happened?' said Derek.

'Got a puncture. Lend me yours. I'll be too late.'

'Get up behind. We'll need us both to climb the wall. There mayn't be a ladder this time.'

Without a word David climbed on to the saddle. Derek stood on the pedals and drove the bike on through the dark. They leaned the bike against the wall where the ivy grew. It still wasn't thick enough to climb, but it was something to get a bit of a grip on. David stood on the saddle of the bike. Derek put his hands under his heels and heaved him up, grunting with the effort, till David could grip the coping of the wall. He still couldn't pull himself right up, but he found a bit of a foothold in the ivy and hung there while Derek climbed on to the cross-bar, steadied himself, and let David use his shoulder as a step. A heave, a scrabble, and he was on the wall.

Derek stood on the saddle and reached up. He couldn't look, but felt David reach down to touch his hand, perhaps just to say goodbye. Derek gripped the hand and held. David heaved. Scrabbling and stretching, Derek leaped for the coping. He heard the bike clatter away beneath him. David's other hand grabbed his collar. He had an elbow on the coping, and now a knee, and he was up.

'Thanks,' he muttered.

The drop on the far side was into blackness. There could have been anything below, but there seemed no help for it. You just had to hang from the coping, let go and trust to luck. Derek landed on softness but wasn't ready for the impact and stumbled, banging his head against the wall. He sat down, his whole skull filled with the pain of it. Dimly he heard a sort of crash, and as the pain seeped away worked out that David must have fallen into a bush. More cracks and rustles as David struggled free.

'Are you OK?' came his voice.

'Think so. Hit my head.'

'Where are you?'

'I'm OK. Let's get on.'

They struggled out through a sort of shrubbery, making enough noise, it seemed, to wake all Hampshire. Derek's head was just sore on the outside now.

Blood was running down his cheek. David was already running, a dark limping shape about twenty yards away. His leg must have gone duff again after all that effort. Derek followed him across the moonlit slopes and levels. They made no effort to hide. If anyone had been watching from the house they must have seen them, the moonlight was so strong. At last they stood panting by the fence of the spring. The rim of shadow still made a thin line under a wall.

'Done it,' whispered David. 'I thought I was stuck.'

'What'd have happened?'

'Don't know.'

'What's it like . . . the other side?'

'Different. Sh.'

The shadow vanished and the reflection of the moon moved on to the troubled disc. Derek glanced sideways at his brother's face. The rippled, reflected light glimmered across it, making it very strange, grey-white like a mushroom, and changing all the time as the ripples changed, as if it wasn't even sure of its own proper shape.

David climbed the fence, grasped the bottom rail and lowered his legs into the water. Derek climbed too, gripped David's hand and crouched to lower his brother – yes, his brother still – his last yard in this world. David let go of the rail and dropped. Derek gripped his hand all the way to the water.

As he felt that silvery touch the movement stopped, and they hung there, either side of the rippled mirror. David didn't seem to want to let go, either.

Different? thought Derek. Different how?

The hand wriggled, impatient. Something must be happening the other side. No time to make up his mind. He let go of the rail.

In the instant that he plunged towards the water he felt a sort of movement around him, very slight, but clear. It was the whole world closing in, filling the gap where he had been. In that instant, he realized everything changed. Jackie would still be at home, Fran would be asleep in his room, not needing to share with Cindy. Nobody would shout at him to come to breakfast. His parents would go about their day with no sense of loss; Jimmy Grove would keep no place for him on the school bus; Mum would be a director of her company, with a car of her own . . . and all the photographs in the albums would show the same cheerful family, two parents, three daughters, no gap, not even the faintest shadow that might once have been Derek.

He was leaving a world where he had never been born.

Almost a Ghost Story

ROBERT WESTALL

'Is the abbey really haunted?' asked Rachel.

'Well, there's the ghost of the nun,' teased Mum.

'Rubbish,' said Dad, without taking his eyes off the road. 'What would a nun be doing in a *monastery*?'

'There's the Nun's Grave,' said Mum, leading him on. And getting him on his high horse, like she always could.

'It's been proved, time and again, that the Nun's Grave's an eighteenth-century folly. Bits of the old church dug up and stuck together to improve the view from the squire's drawing-room windows. They've excavated it three times – nothing but black-beetles.' He changed gear grumpily. The long drive-way to the abbey had become very bumpy. The headlights turned it into a series of miniature mountains and black caverns.

A tall grey shape with upstretched arms glowed dimly into view, far away; grew and grew till every

last twig glistened white against the darkness; then, when it seemed about to engulf them, whirled away overhead. Then another, and another. Once, said Dad, there'd been a whole avenue of beech trees, but each winter gale left fresh gaps. Huge beech-corpses lay at intervals, shorn of their branches by power-saws.

'All the same,' said Mum, 'it feels funny, coming back after all this time. How long has it stood empty?'

'Twenty years – since the country club closed. I was there when it happened – we were under drinking-age, but they were letting in anybody with money at the end. Anyway, the barman dropped a crate of beer in the upstairs bar, and the beer trickled down through the floorboards and blew all the wiring. You ought to have seen the sparks. We thought we were all going up in a blue light – we never stopped running till we reached Davenham. Club closed straight after . . .' Dad laughed to himself, at the memory of being a young rip; he was never cross for long. But Mum couldn't leave him alone.

'Perhaps the nun disapproved of all that boozing . . .'

'*Rubbish*! That electric wiring must've come out of the ark. It's just that they tried to turn the abbey into so many things – Civil Defence Centre, school for accountants – none of them prospered.'

His voice trailed off. The gaunt beeches continued to appear and whirl overhead. Rachel snuggled up tight behind Mum and Dad's shoulders. It was suddenly cold, dark and lonely in the back of the

Maxi. There was a draught and a rattle from the right-hand door.

'Daddy, my door's not shut properly . . .'

Dad reached behind him without stopping, opened the door and slammed it solidly. That made Rachel feel better. So did the string of car rear-lights in front; the distant headlights behind, bouncing wildly into the sky as the following cars hit the cart-ruts in the drive. Rachel was glad they weren't alone.

'It's a good place for a Christmas concert,' said Mum, snuggling down into her fur collar with an enjoyable shiver. 'With a ghost an' all . . .'

'The new owners are desperate for funds. Place is full of dry rot. They say that upstairs the hardboard partitions are buckled with it, like a shell had hit them. And down in the cellars, it grows out of the walls like an old man's beard.'

'D'you think it'll be safe?' asked Mum, suddenly really worried.

'*You* bought the tickets. *You* wanted the thrill!'

'I don't want to break me ankle.'

'That's more likely than any flippin' ghost.'

'Were the monks good men?' asked Rachel, suddenly.

'Bunch of layabouts,' Dad snorted. 'Lived a life of idle luxury. Tried to build a church bigger'n Westminster Abbey – for only twenty of them – only the walls blew down in a great storm, afore they got the roof on, an' that was that. But they still went on squeezing their tenants for every penny they had. Tenants murdered one monk, an' played football wi' his head.'

'Oh,' said Rachel.

'That nun,' said Mum dreamily. 'The book said she fell in love with the wicked Abbot an' pined away.'

'That book was the worst Victorian novel ever written. Ever tried reading it?'

'Only the first five pages. Then I skipped, looking for juicy bits.'

'Find any?'

Mum shook her head as they swung on to the rough grassy car-park.

'Looks funny, all lit up,' said Dad. 'I came past it many a time, in me courting days, an' never a light but the moon glinting on the windows.'

'You never brought me,' said Mum.

'Where's the Nun's Grave?' asked Rachel.

'I'll show you,' said Dad, glancing at his watch and getting his big rubber torch out of the glove compartment. 'We've got five minutes before it starts.'

'Not me,' shivered Mum. 'Give me the tickets and I'll keep your seats.'

Dad and Rachel walked down the great dark side of the abbey; the grass was so frosty it scrunched under their feet.

'Them's the Abbot's chimneys,' said Dad, nodding upwards. Rachel stared up at the great black hexagons, towering above the roofline.

'How long have the abbots been gone?'

'Henry the Eighth got shot of them – sold the house to the Holcrofts. It passed from hand to hand after that – nobody kept it long. Last real owner went to farm in Kenya in 1940. Then it was a prisoner-of-war camp – Jerries. Anyway, here's your so-called *grave*.'

He shone the torch. There was a hexagonal stone base, then a square pillar, then a little stone house on top, with a figure sitting in the arch. In the torchlight, Rachel could see that the figure's hands and face had been worn away by wind and rain. And yet, as Dad flicked the torch contemptuously around, you could almost make out a little face . . . nose and eyes . . . but they changed, as the light flickered.

'She's got a head-dress like a nun!'

'All ladies wore them, in those days. C'mon, or your mum'll be having a fit.'

There was a man on the door, in overcoat, hat and muffler up to his ears. He waved them through, with a mumble through the muffler, because Mum had explained about the tickets. They were in a long, long vaulted corridor, colder than outside. It had been painted a filthy bright orange by the owners of the country club, but that made it more spooky, not less. Like Dracula wearing make-up.

'There's the Ladies, in case you need it,' said Dad. They walked on and on, under the orange vaults and weak buzzing neons, past the black, black windows.

'This was the monks' cloister,' said Dad.

They finally came to another man in coat, hat and muffler, at the foot of the grand staircase. There was a wooden gargoyle sitting on the newelpost, half-lion, half-dragon. It watched Rachel with sly dark carved eyes as if waiting for a chance to bite her. There was a faint hum of human voices, trickling down the stair-well.

From the safety of the stairs, Rachel looked back, trying to see the sign for the Ladies. The far end of the cloister seemed lost in a thin black mist, as if somebody had left a window open, and let the dark in.

The great hall was full; a sea of fur coats, fur hats, suede boots. Nobody was taking anything off, for small draughts curled round your legs like icy snakes, every time a late comer opened the hall doors. They found Mum nicely-placed by a huge fireplace that looked like a Gothic tombstone, complete with a pair of winged figures that certainly weren't angels. It was extravagantly filled with a roaring log fire. Some of the logs were three feet long.

'Central heating's not much cop,' said Mum. 'I'm roasting one side and freezing the other. Let's cuddle up, George. Put Rachel in the middle.'

They'd no sooner settled than a tall thin grey-haired man rose to his feet across the sea of fur hats. People eventually stopped losing and finding their gloves, talking, and waving to friends, and settled to listen. As the gentleman had floppy hair and a great sheaf of papers, and had to keep pushing his hair out of his eyes and retrieving papers from the floor, he was not easy to listen to. But it appeared he was the secretary of the charity that had bought the abbey. They hoped to turn it into a children's home. They had saved the abbey from the very brink of disaster; pulled eight-foot ash trees out of cracks in its walls; spent all one stormy night on the roof, holding down the slates with their outspread bodies.

'Otherwise you wouldn't be sitting here tonight . . .'

A lot of fur hats tilted, as people looked nervously at the ceiling. It certainly carried a lot of peculiar spreading stains, like maps of South America and Norway.

'I think we can guarantee your safety this evening,' said the secretary, and dropped his notes again. There was an anxious titter, thin as the blowing of dead leaves on an autumn night.

He told them of the charity's first night in the abbey, with ninety-one locked rooms and only ninety keys. How all the lights failed half an hour after dusk; how his bedroom was nearly a hundred yards from the kitchen.

'But we learnt that night that there are either no ghosts in the abbey, or, if there are, they are friendly to our cause, and want the abbey to survive. So I think they would be pleased to see us all gathered here tonight, a week before Christmas, so that the old house is alive again . . .'

Then the musicians walked in. Three plump young men in crumpled dinner-jackets, with dark crinkly hair and horn-rimmed spectacles. They might have been brothers. And a very elegant lady with long neck and long graceful bare arms, who was going to play the cello. They announced themselves as the Rococo Ensemble, and began plucking and tweaking nervously at their violins and double-bass. The swan-necked lady became visibly aware of the temperature in the hall and the writhing icy snakes from the doors, which kept opening and shutting in the draught, as if someone kept meaning to come in, then changed their mind. Rachel watched the lady's arms and neck turn first purple and then blue, in interesting patches; saw the lady look longingly at the thick woolly stole at her feet, then decide that one could not really play the cello wearing a stole . . .

Then their leader announced they would begin with one of Vivaldi's 'Four Seasons' and they had decided to make it . . . 'Winter' . . .

More thin laughter. Then the four musicians looked at each other with raised eyebrows and cold little smiles, and were off.

And it was very fine; but very wintry. Rachel's eyes swept the ceiling in a dream. Huge oak beams soared to the top of the roof . . . 'The wicked Abbot's original beams,' said Dad in a whisper. In between, later families had plastered their coats of arms, boasting who'd married whom. But Rachel wasn't much bothered by who'd married whom. She had not liked that phrase about the old house coming back to life. Her mind roamed round the house. The ancient central heating system, passing through wall after wall, from darkened room to darkened room, hissing hot water and steam and totally failing to keep the cold at bay. The black attics, where the partitions were buckled as if a shell had hit them. The long orange cloister that led to the loo, full of smoky dark at the far end; the cellars where the dry rot grew out of the walls like an old man's beard . . .

And all the time Vivaldi's music of raindrops pattered on their ears, and the air grew colder. Only the ceiling looked warm, lit with a rich yellow light, from concealed spotlights hidden behind the beams.

The music ended; the musicians almost ran for the comfort of their changing-room and its two-bar electric fire. The secretary announced that the buffet was now open in the state dining-room, with a choice of wine or hot coffee. There was nearly a stampede, scarcely checked by middle class decorum.

The state dining-room was fabulous. A huge white marble fireplace with columns, a huge white door with columns, and a white and gilt plaster ceiling. Pity there was a gaping black hole in the ceiling, with a raw new wooden post thrust up through it, high as a fir tree. The secretary announced that it was dry rot, but perfectly well in hand. Somebody had pinned a blue notice to the post, saying 'Queue here for coffee'.

The state dining-table was smothered in mini pork pies, chicken croquettes and huge cream gateaux from end to end.

'Good spread,' said Dad, handing yellow paper plates around.

'The plates are very small,' said Mum. 'That won't hold much!'

'You can come round again.'

'What, after this bunch of vultures have been through it? Anyway, those sausage rolls have been kept warm too long – they're all shrivelled.'

'That table's a lovely bit of mahogany.'

'You can't eat mahogany!'

Rachel went round again three times, and had two cups of very hot coffee. Then the standing up and the cold and the two cups of coffee began to make their effects felt. She knew she ought to go to the loo.

Then she thought about the misty orange cloister . . .

'Mum – do you want the loo? I know where it is.'

'Shhh – in public – certainly not. These vol-au-vents aren't bad, George. Try one.'

Rachel desperately kept her legs pressed together. Once they sat down again she'd be all right.

'Will you please take your seats again, ladies and gentlemen.'

'Mum – I've got to go . . .'

'Go on, then. Hurry up – it's starting. Trust *you* . . .'

'Come with me?'

'Certainly not. You're a big girl now – nearly twelve.'

There was no choice. Rachel went. Running down the Grand Staircase she met a few people coming up, stamping out their cigarettes on the stone, then picking up the flattened dog-ends guiltily and putting them in their breast pockets. Still, there was still the man on the door, at the far end of the cloister . . . he'd be sort of company.

She met him hurrying up the stairs too, blowing on his hands and very glad to leave his lonely post. She was now quite alone.

She began walking along the cloister, towards the mist of dark. She couldn't bear to look at it. She walked on, counting the cracks between the paving-stones instead. But she had to look up, eventually.

There was a black-robed figure, standing right out-side the entrance to the Ladies. Black from head to foot, and its back turned towards her. Absolutely still.

Terror transfixed Rachel. Then the figure moved slightly, and the black robe lifted a little from the floor, to reveal a pair of sparkling diamante heels.

Blood surged back into Rachel's heart in great pain-ful pumps. No nun ever wore *diamanté* heels. The figure turned, to reveal a plump lady in black velvet evening cloak and sequinned dress, with a kind face and dangly earrings. She gave a start when she saw Rachel, then smiled.

'Oh, you did make me jump! Isn't this a funny old place? Which way is it back? I'm quite lost.'

'If you wait for me a tick,' said Rachel desperately, 'I'll show you.'

The woman smiled understandingly.

Rachel had never been so quick in her life.

Things really began to go wrong in the second half. The musicians tried over and over again to get their instruments tuned properly, and couldn't seem to manage it.

'It's the cold,' said Dad. 'It affects the catgut.'

'It's affecting my guts,' said Mum. 'I wish now I'd gone with our Rachel.'

More in desperation than hope, the musicians launched off into some Albinoni, with a half-hearted little quip about hot rhythms. Albinoni would not have liked it. The two violins could not get together, and wowed frequently and horribly. The swan-necked lady had donned not only her stole, but also a clashing polo-neck sweater, and it showed in her playing. The double-bass, stout backstop, seemed somehow to get detached; its sound seemed to be coming from one corner of the rafters.

'Funny acoustics,' whispered Dad. 'Must be a layer of warm air up there.'

'You must be joking,' said Mum. 'I've just lost my last layer of warm air, and I won't tell you where from. There's no *heat* in this fire.'

Rachel held forward her hand, and it was true. The fire roared up the chimney as fiercely as ever, but not a trace of heat could she feel. All, musicians and audience, seemed locked in some terrible refrigerator.

And then, up among the rafters and the ceiling spotlights, Rachel saw a little black dancing shadow, moving up and down erratically, like a flake of soot from a burning chimney; like a little black butterfly.

She watched it uneasily for a bit, then tugged Dad's sleeve.

'Moth,' said Dad. 'Been hibernating. Been wakened up by the heat of the spotlights.'

'What heat?' asked Mum, from the depths of her collar.

Rachel forgot the music, went on watching the moth. There was a funny effect. As it fluttered nearer the spotlights, seeking light and warmth, the spotlights threw its shadow on the ceiling, magnified many times. The shadow looked as big as a bird, waxing and waning, depending where the moth flew.

And then it seemed that the moth itself, the solid black shape, became as big as its shadow, and the shadow grew many times bigger. Big as a person.

People began to notice. Little indrawn breaths came from the women; then little shrieks as the thing came lower, with wavering uncertain flight. The music flew wilder and wilder, as even the musicians turned their heads to follow its flight, without stopping playing.

Suddenly, it was hovering right in front of Rachel's face. Black, black like a robe, with a little bit of white and paleness on top.

She stared and stared and stared . . .

Then Dad's arm crashed across, with his open tweed cap in his fist. It hit the black thing a terrible sideways blow, and flung it into the heart of the roaring flames in the great Gothic fireplace. There it hovered a moment, still fluttering to live. Then there was a puff of dark grey smoke, and a slight and evil smell, and it was quite gone.

'Bloody bat,' said Dad, uncomfortably, as everyone

turned to stare at him. 'Nasty bloody things. Good riddance to bad rubbish.'

Then Rachel was crying uncontrollably. Dad tried shaking her; Mum tried cuddling her. But it was no good.

Guiltily they led her towards the doors that still opened and closed a little in the draught, as if someone was trying to get in and failing.

The tall grey man tried to apologize. 'Nests in the chimneys . . . nearly smoked us out this morning . . . early days.'

But no one could hear him, because Rachel would not stop crying.

Audience and musicians watched them go, sympathetically.

At the door, Rachel broke away, back into the room.

'But didn't you *see*,' she shouted. 'It had a human face! It wanted me to help her. Didn't you *see*?'

The doors closed behind her, as Mum and Dad dragged her out.

'Poor child – quite overwrought.'

'She's had a nasty fright – very nasty.'

'They're very imaginative at that age . . .'

The Albinoni picked up wearily, like a record-player switched on when a record has been left half-played. The audience settled back into its fur coats and suede boots, to weather out the concert.

But there was never another concert in that abbey.

The Passing of Puddy

GENE KEMP

'That's it. That's it, Puddy, me old moggy, you're gumming away nicely,' crooned my brother, Jed, from his kneeling position on the kitchen floor, black leather rear end stuck high in the air, black spiky hair tangling with Puddy's dirty fur.

And Puddy was gumming away very well indeed considering his great age, a hundred and seventy-five at the last count, seven of his years to one of ours, an old, old pussy cat, thin with arthritic legs so he could no longer jump the back wall as he used to, and all his teeth worn down to stumps after years of fierce and terrible hunting: mice, sparrows, blackbirds, gerbils, hamsters, even once a crow, and even more remarkable a grey bird, with shining blue feathers under its wings, a jay said my mother. Those grey and blue feathers were scattered from one end of the house to the other by the time Puddy had finished with it. You name it, Puddy caught it.

But now he was old, thin in limb and stumpy of tooth and my vile brother had carefully laid some tired pieces of French garlic sausage, sliced very fine, with orange plastic round the edges, you know the kind, on the kitchen floor where they stuck to the worn red quarry tiles, wringing wet because it'd been raining for days, and then they sweat, just as Puddy was sweating with the effort of trying to detach the meat from them – if cats sweat, that is – with no teeth to speak of and my brother Jed sweating with delight just watching him.

'Don't be so filthy mean,' I shrieked, seizing a bit of garlic sausage, very smelly it was, and shoving it into Puddy's eager mouth, whereupon he almost choked with joy.

And a voice came from the door. We had been joined.

'That cat ought to be put down. It's a health hazard,' said my half-brother, Colin, standing there in his grass-hopper-green track suit, oozing health and vitality, just having been jogging. Fourteen thirty hours was always jog time with Colin.

Jed rose up slowly.

'Nobody, but nobody ain't gonna put that cat up, down or through any place else.'

'Everybody knows it's not healthy keeping a cat as old as that and in rotten condition. Besides it's cruelty.'

Jed's spikes sharpened and shone black purple against the light of the window. Puddy continued to gum away furiously at the bits of garlic sausage.

'You looking for trouble?' asked Jed. ''Cos if you ain't, you're finding it just the same.'

They were about the same height, Jed whippet thin, Colin stocky in the track suit.

'I might just ring the RSPCA,' he said.

'And if you do you might just be needing it yourself,' Jed's voice would have chilled the freezer.

Me, I am just a natural born coward and I hate rows, so I picked up Puddy and his garlic sausage (they got together happily and smellily) before the horrible duo started on each other, but at that moment Mum arrived saying either help or get out, there's a lot on tonight, so it's an early meal, Jess – that's me – get on with the veg and Jed, there are at least four of your mates in the hall drinking coffee and playing gin rummy so get rid of them, and Colin wake up your mother, she's bound to be having a rest somewhere, and find Dilly and Dally. And put the cat outside, Jess. It needs fresh air.

Aroma of garlic was spreading fragrantly all around the kitchen, pongy at the best of times, ever since my mother put too much fertilizer on the herbs and they grew to the size of cabbages, and also since Jed took up Indian cooking with no talent for it.

'That cat doesn't need fresh air, it needs a miracle,' muttered Colin, with unusual wit for him.

'So do we all,' snapped Mum with more than edge to her voice.

So I put the cat outside, made some coffee and got stuck into the vast mound of veg required for an evening meal in this house, thinking bitterly how life had changed since Colin, Dilly, Dally and Caroline, their mother, had arrived. Out of all recognition, in fact. We'd always had lots of people around but now, all the cosy chats over coffee, the easy atmosphere had gone as Mum grew bossier, Jed stroppier, and I turned into an unpaid, low grade assistant cook, vegetable peeler, coffee maker and child-minder.

What a set-up. My father married Caroline – it was all very posh – but after Colin was born he pushed off with her cousin, who just happened to be my mum. Some time after Jed was born, Dad and Mum got hitched and I arrived and then later once again Dad pushed off. Not a man you could rely on, Mum said. We stayed together as a one parent family, which suited Mum apparently. But six weeks ago, who should turn up at the doorway, weeping picturesquely on something that turned out to be Colin, with two little girls just behind them, but Caroline. Second hubby had turned very nasty, and having seen Mum's name in the paper on account of her work in the community, and being her cousin into the bargain where else could she go? Jed, having taken one look at them, suggested a few places but Mum, believing as she does in the sisterhood of womanhood, welcomed them all in.

'Why do all your men push off?' I wanted to know, but no one answered.

'I've had a terrible time, darling,' sobbed Caroline over her third glass of gin, 'but I know you'll look after me and my rights. And you won't mind Nanas will you?'

Because worst of all, Caroline had brought her dog. A yappy, hairy thing called Bananas.

'Bananas,' choked Jed, rolling about the floor. 'Bananas,' and he was off again. After a time he recovered and called the cat.

'Kill, Puddy, kill,' he instructed.

And Puddy nearly did just that despite his tooth shortage. Dilly and Dally, weeping, rushed their mother in to save him. Mum followed.

'No darrling,' wept Caroline, 'I've never been one to complain but that Monster of Sadism and his beastly animal will be the death of poor wee beautiful Nanas if Something Isn't Done.'

Mother's success lies in the fact that she always knows what's to be done, and she soon came up with the answer.

'Jess,' she said. I was bathing Bananas' nose, now the size of a light bulb as Caroline felt faint and the twins didn't know how. 'Jess,' she repeated as I tried not to hear. 'Do something about the dog.'

In the end I fixed him with a box in the shed, and made a kind of run with bits of board and rope. Then I pinned up his exercise rota in the kitchen and told everybody to read it. Nobody took any notice. I was the only one to take him for a walk, though I kept telling Colin that jogging was good for animals.

Then Puddy turned peculiar – even more than usual, I mean. He made little rushes up and down pretending to chase things and made himself so giddy he kept falling over. He found a ball of wool nearly as old as he was and patted it coyly, peering at us out of the corner of his wicked old eyes to see if we were watching him being a pretty puddicat. He took to rubbing round legs and purring.

'What on earth's got into him?' asked Mum angrily. 'He nearly made me scald myself making the tea this morning.'

'He's pretending he's a kitten all over again,' explained Jed. 'He's trying to be lovable. Idiot Puddy. I don't suppose you were lovable even when you *were* a kitten.'

'But why?' I asked.

'You're slow. Because of the dog, of course. He's afraid he might have to go. You're safe, Puddepha. The swines shall never get rid of you.'

'Talking about yourself as usual?' Colin had arrived.

Mum stopped that fight by hauling them apart by their ears. A big woman, my mum.

The following day Puddy laid three dead mice on Caroline's bed, and a dead hamster on each of the twins'. *Their* hamsters.

'How can we stay in this Cruel, Heartless Household?' cried Caroline, while the twins wailed in the background. Jed sprang to the door.

'Don't let me stop you. Feel free to leave at any time. I'll help you pack.'

But they still stayed.

'Why?' I asked. 'They don't like us and they know we don't like them.'

'They've no money and nowhere to go, and they're my kith and kin, and whither they go, I shall go —' Mum began.

'You've got it all wrong,' Jed said. 'You always do when you go Biblical.'

'I had a very Biblical upbringing, remember. Not like you lot.'

'Yes, and it's made a saint of you, Mo,' Jed went on, being always cheekier with her than I was. 'As for that lot, parasitical layabouts, as long as it's all free and they can eat your cooking and she doesn't have to stir her idle self to do anything, then they'll stay as long as we let 'em. But I'm gonna get rid of 'em. You see. I'll find a way.'

'I half agree with you,' said Mum, sounding tired for once.

The atmosphere in our house grew even more strained. Even the weather was awful. At last, it stopped raining, the sun came out, and it felt like summer so I rang up my friend Zoe and we went swimming. I returned home feeling great cos I got whistled at. That great feeling lasted till I turned into our street. I could hear the row at our house from the corner. I ran.

Jed and Colin were battling in the hall, Dilly and Dally were kicking Jed, and above it all Caroline was shouting, 'I'll ring for the police. I'll ring for the police.'

I managed to get the receiver off her, and wondered what the heck to do for there was no sign of Mum and I couldn't cope with all the loonies. But I had to. There wasn't anybody else, only me, the world's greatest coward. I ran to the kitchen, filled a bucket with water, squirted in some washing-up liquid, ran back to the hall and threw all of it over all of them.

'Jolly good,' said Mum right behind me. 'You're learning. Only make it pepper next time. Less damage to the house. Shut up, you lot.'

They shut up, even Caroline, bubbles rising from her new hair set.

'What happened? Jed?'

'Puddy . . .' he stood and shook with dripping water and laughter.

'I knew that cat would be mixed up in it somewhere . . .'

'It's not funny,' shouted Colin.

'It's disgusting!' shrieked Caroline.

'What is?' I yelled.

'Puddy . . . Puddy . . .' Jed spluttered. 'Made a mess in Colin's training boots and Colin didn't realize and put them on.'

'AND WE'RE LEAVING!' shouted Caroline.

My mother started to laugh and laugh and tears rained down her face. At last she quietened down. I waited.

'Jess,' she said. 'Put the cat out and make some coffee.' I knew it.

But still they didn't go. There was always yet

another good reason for putting off their departure. A sneaky, early autumn wind whipped yellowing leaves up the street. The summer heat had gone.

'The holidays are nearly over,' Jed muttered as we crashed out listening to Pink Floyd.

'Wasn't much of a holiday. And they're still there.'

'But not for long, Jess. I've got an idea.'

'Tell me.'

'No, it'll work better if you haven't a clue. Just follow any lead I give and don't let on a thing. OK?'

'OK.'

It was quiet at home these days, even Puddy keeping out of trouble. So quiet was he, in fact, that he didn't turn up to his evening meal. I didn't worry because he'd stayed out before, especially in his courting days though at age one hundred and seventy-five he was getting a bit past that now. By the next day, though, I was worried, went round to inform any neighbours that might care, put an ad in the paper and walked up and down the street carrying his food bowl crammed with raw liver, shouting 'Puddy' and feeling an idiot. Caroline and company kept fairly silent, though Colin kept grinning. Jed walked about the house, black and sombre as an undertaker.

'If anything's been done to that cat, I'll see they suffer the torments of Hell,' he remarked over Mum's glorious Lancashire hotpot.

'Shut up,' she said. 'Puddy will probably turn up in all good time. He has before, and if he doesn't, well, he's a very old cat and has had a good innings. He may have gone away to die quietly without any fuss, you know, for he was never a fussy cat.'

Jed leapt into the air, shaking his fists (and the table and the plates of hotpot), and slammed out of the room, turning and catching my eye as he left. And I cottoned on. I might be slow but I always got there in the end. I didn't mention it when I spotted him coming out of the Joke Shop with a parcel under his arm, though I couldn't resist whispering, 'I know. Where have you got him?' later that day.

'Belt up,' he snarled, eyes green glass chips. I didn't mind. I'd got the message. But how was Jed going to manage it, I wondered.

The house felt like a morgue or what I imagine a morgue feels like. And we waited. Waited for something somewhere to happen. Like something about to burst. After a time I couldn't bear this any longer, so I rang up my friend Zoe and we went to the pictures. And it was a horror film all about this family trapped in a haunted house.

'That was horrible,' said Zoe, as we walked home. 'It really scared the living daylights out of me.'

'Seemed phoney to me.'

'How would you know?'

'You'd be surprised. But I just know it wasn't really frightening.'

As soon as I stepped in my house I knew what I'd meant, for here was the real thing. Fear gathered me up, so that I could hardly breathe. Jed, how do you do it? I thought, as I ran to the kitchen for company. You're a genius. They'll never be able to stand this. It's nearly too much for me and I know it's all a trick. They were all seated round the table waiting for me. And a tin of Kit-e-Kat leapt off the shelf and rolled across the floor. Caroline screeched.

'Who did that?' cried Colin.

'It's beginning,' Jed moaned in one of those doom-laden voices.

'What do you mean?' cried Colin. Mum came out of the pantry where she'd been getting some dishes.

'Look, let's get on. Some of us have work to do this evening. Jess pick up that tin, will you?'

It was after twelve when Caroline arose, pale and fragile with dark rings round her eyes. She was sorry but she could only manage a Tiny cup of Weak Tea.

'What's the matter now?' asked my mother who seemed to be irritable all of the time instead of part of the time.

'Never has anyone suffered from such Awful Night-mares.'

'What sort of awful nightmares?'

'Terrible Grrreat Beasts. Swirling and Looming around poor little me.'

'Beasts?' I saw a beast prowling past my door in the night when I got up to go to the bog,' announced Colin. 'It went in to see the twins.'

'Oh, NO, No, No! Not my Little Ones. Anything but That!' shrilled Caroline. She went to the door and called for them. After a while they came in. Very muddy they were. Caroline clasped them to her.

'I wish you wouldn't do that,' said Dally wriggling free.

'My darrlings! Did you . . . were there . . . did you have Bad Dreams last night? Tell your mummy. Don't be Afraid.'

'No, we didn't have nightmares. Puddy came and sat on our beds. In turn.'

'Puddy?' Caroline's voice rose to a shriek. 'Puddy came? He's still alive then?'

'Oh no. Puddy dead.'

'He sat on Dally's bed first, then Dilly's. Can we go now? We're having a lovely funeral.'

'Funeral? Do you mean Puddy's Funeral?' screeched Caroline.

'No, Teddy's funeral. He died in the night. So we buried him. Bye-bye.'

'Oh, I can't Stand this,' cried their mother.

It's all going well, I thought. Everything's helping. Just wish it wasn't so cold . . . and spooky, though.

Colin's yells woke us at midnight. Mum and I arrived together. He was absolutely scared rigid and for the first time I felt sorry for him.

'It's only Bananas howling,' explained Mum as if she was talking to the twins. 'It's nothing to be afraid of. Your mother took him to bed with her for company and he doesn't seem to like it much . . .'

That was the understatement of the year. Bananas

was wailing like an ambulance speeding through a crowded city.

'. . . but it's nothing to worry about, so just go to sleep.'

'It's not that,' he trembled. 'A great cat face keeps appearing at the bottom of my bed and miaowing at me.'

'There's nothing there, you know,' said Mum gently. 'I'll leave your door open and the landing light on. Then you'll be all right. Good night, Colin.'

'G-g-good night.' His teeth chattered but he slid down into bed.

Mum paused outside my door.

'You know Jess, I've got the feeling there's something fishy going on.'

'Nothing . . . fishy, Mum.'

'I expect it's just me imagining things.'

I felt that I wanted to tell her there and then, that I needed all her common sense, but Jed's been funny before if I've told what was supposed to be hush-hush.

'It'll be all right,' I said.

'I hope so. I'd hate to think it was just me going nutty.'

'Not you, Mum. Night.'

'Good night, Jess.'

I thought I couldn't possibly get to sleep but I did.

'Are you going jogging today?' I asked at breakfast. 'I thought I might come with you.'

Colin shook his head. 'I don't feel fit enough.'

'You mustn't mind Puddy visiting you at night. It's nothing to be upset about. Now he's a ghost he can't make messes in your boots any more. What's the matter? You are a funny colour.'

'That bloody cat!' cried Colin, standing up and knocking his chair over. I'd never heard him swear before.

'I told you something would happen if you harmed him,' said Jed, sounding like Judge Jeffreys on a good hanging day.

'But I didn't. I never touched him,' shouted Colin, rushing from the room.

That night a force eight gale surged through the mad skies, hurling dustbins, flinging down aerials, tossing tiles contemptuously off roofs. And tomorrow's the last day of the holidays, I thought, watching the telly screen flicker. For once we were all watching together, even the dog. No one had put the twins to bed. No one seemed to want to move. I know I didn't fancy being on my own at all.

I wonder what Jed will get up to next, I thought, looking at him, but he was absolutely still, and at that moment the screen blanked, and the sound stopped. Outside the wind dropped abruptly and in the unexpected silence could be heard the sound of Puddy wailing wildly right above our heads. Bananas lifted up his head and howled.

The doorbell rang. Everybody jumped, except my mother. 'Jess,' she said. Despite being the world's worst coward, I answered the door. A man stood there.

'Does a Mrs Caroline . . .?' He got no further. I was nearly knocked down in the rush.

'Darrling, oh darrling Peter! You've come! To take us home. Away from here. Away from this Horrible Haunted House,' shrieked Caroline, wrapping herself all round him.

'Dad, am I glad to see you,' cried Colin.

I helped them pack.

'But I don't want to leave Puddy,' protested Dally. I'd always liked her better than Dilly.

'Come on, lend a hand,' I said to Jed, who was sitting there as though carved out of marble. 'They're leaving. You've done it.' He didn't stir.

'Oh well, be like that,' I said as I went to wave them off. Mum had been called out on a late night problem. I made some coffee and took it in to Jed. 'You genius.' I tried to kiss him. He pushed me off.

'You idiot,' he replied. 'Don't you understand? I didn't do anything, only pull that Kit-e-Kat tin with a bit of cotton. Then Puddy took over . . .' His face crumpled. I felt terrible. 'And Jess, I'm absolutely scared silly of ghosts, even the ghost of Puddy. What are we gonna do?'

I knew what I'd got to do, me, the world's worst coward. With the wild wind shouting and raving all round, and Puddy miaowing from every window in the house, I searched the garden, until I found his body hidden in the undergrowth by the wall at the back of the garden. When I'd buried him, I bent my head and said the Our Father, which came first to mind, and then, right out of the blue from my Infant school, Now I Lay Me Down To Sleep. The miaowing was fainter now, and because I was pretty knackered, I said, 'For Heaven's sake, Puddy, be a good cat and do just that.' The wind dropped and silence settled.

I got back just in time to make coffee for Mum who'd just arrived. 'Worn out,' she said. 'Me, too,' I said. 'You can't be, you're young,' she grinned.

We never saw or heard anything of Puddy again.

Humblepuppy

JOAN AIKEN

Our house was furnished mainly from auction sales. When you buy furniture that way you get a lot of extra things besides the particular piece that you were after, since the stuff is sold in lots: Lot 13, two Persian rugs, a set of golf-clubs, a sewing-machine, a walnut radio cabinet, and a plinth.

It was in this way that I acquired a tin deedbox, which came with two coal-scuttles and a broom cupboard. The deed-box is solid metal, painted black, big as a medium-sized suitcase. When I first brought it home I put it in my study, planning to use it as a kind of filing cabinet for old typescripts. I had gone into the kitchen, and was busy arranging the brooms in their new home, when I heard a loud thumping coming from the direction of the study.

I went back, thinking that a bird must have flown through the window; no bird, but the banging seemed to be inside the deed-box. I had already opened it as

soon as it was in my possession, to see if there were diamonds or bearer bonds worth thousands of pounds inside (there weren't), but I opened it again. The key was attached to the handle by a thin chain. There was nothing inside. I shut it. The banging started again. I opened it.

Still nothing inside.

Well, this was broad daylight, two o'clock on Thursday afternoon, people going past in the road outside and a radio schools programme chatting away to itself in the next room. It was not a ghostly kind of time, so I put my hand into the empty box and moved it about.

Something shrank away from my hand. I heard a faint, scared whimper. It could almost have been my own, but wasn't. Knowing that someone – something? – else was afraid too put heart into me. Exploring carefully and gently around the interior of the box I felt the contour of a small, bony, warm, trembling body with big awkward feet, and silky dangling ears, and a cold nose that, when I found it, nudged for a moment anxiously but trustingly into the palm of my hand. So I knelt down, put the other hand into the box as well, cupped them under a thin little ribby chest, and lifted out Humblepuppy.

He was quite light.

I couldn't see him, but I could hear his faint inquiring whimper, and I could hear his toe-nails scratch on the floor-boards.

Just at that moment the cat, Taffy, came in.

Taffy has a lot of character. Every cat has a lot of character, but Taffy has more than most, all of it inconvenient. For instance, although he is very sociable, and longs for company, he just despises company in the form of dogs. The mere sound of a dog barking two streets away is enough to make his fur stand up like a porcupine's quills and his tail swell like a mushroom cloud.

Which it did the instant he saw Humblepuppy.

Now here is the interesting thing. I could feel and hear Humblepuppy, but couldn't see him; Taffy, apparently, could see and smell him, but couldn't feel him. We soon discovered this. For Taffy, sinking into a low, gladiator's crouch, letting out all the time a fearsome throaty wauling like a bagpipe revving up its drone, inched his way along to where Humblepuppy huddled trembling by my left foot, and then dealt him what ought to have been a swinging right-handed clip on the ear. 'Get out of my house, you filthy little canine scum!' was what he was plainly intending to convey.

But the swipe failed to connect; instead it landed on my shin.

I've never seen a cat so astonished. It was like watching a kitten meet itself for the first time in a looking-glass. Taffy ran round to the back of where Humblepuppy was sitting; felt; smelt; poked gingerly with a paw; leapt back nervously; crept forward again. All the time Humblepuppy just sat, trembling a little, giving out this faint beseeching sound that meant:

'I'm only a poor little mongrel without a smidgen of harm in me. *Please* don't do anything nasty! I don't even know how I came here.'

It certainly was a puzzle how he had come. I rang the auctioneers (after shutting Taffy *out* of and Humblepuppy *in* to the study with a bowl of water and a handful of Boniebisk, Taffy's favourite breakfast food).

The auctioneers told me that Lot 12, deed-box, coal-scuttles and broom cupboard, had come from Riverland Rectory, where Mr Smythe, the old rector, had lately died aged ninety. Had he ever possessed a dog, or a puppy? They couldn't say; they had merely received instructions from a firm of lawyers to sell the furniture.

I never did discover how poor little Humblepuppy's ghost got into that deed-box. Maybe he was shut in by mistake, long ago, and suffocated; maybe some callous Victorian gardener dropped him, box and all, into a river, and the box was later found and fished out.

Anyway, and whatever had happened in the past, now that Humblepuppy had come out of his box, he was very pleased with the turn his affairs had taken, ready to be grateful and affectionate. As I sat typing I'd often hear a patter-patter, and feel his small chin fit itself comfortably over my foot, ears dangling. Goodness knows what kind of a mixture he was; something between a spaniel and a terrier, I'd guess. In the evening, watching television or sitting by the fire, one would suddenly find his warm weight leaning against one's leg. (He didn't put on a lot of weight while he was with us, but his bony little ribs filled out a bit.)

For the first few weeks we had a lot of trouble with Taffy, who was very surly over the whole business and blamed me bitterly for not getting rid of this low-class intruder. But Humblepuppy was extremely placating, got back into his deed-box whenever the atmosphere became too volcanic, and did his very best not to be a nuisance.

By and by Taffy thawed. As I've said, he is really a very sociable cat. Although quite old, seventy cat years, he dearly likes cheerful company, and generally has some young cat friend who comes to play with him, either in the house or the garden. In the last few years we've had Whisky, the black and white pub cat, who used to sit washing the smell of fish and chips off his fur under the dripping tap in our kitchen sink; Tetanus, the hairdresser's thickset black, who took a fancy to sleeping on top of our china cupboard every night all one winter, and used to startle me very much by jumping down heavily on to my shoulder as I made the breakfast coffee; Sweet Charity, a little grey Persian who came to a sad end under the wheels of a police car; Charity's grey and white stripy cousin Fred, whose owners presently moved from next door to another part of the town.

It was soon after Fred's departure that Humble-puppy arrived, and from my point of view he couldn't have been more welcome. Taffy missed Fred badly, and expected *me* to play with him instead; it was sad to see this large elderly tabby rushing hopefully up and down stairs after breakfast, or hiding behind the armchair and jumping out on to nobody; or howling, howling, howling at me until I escorted him out into the garden, where he'd rush to the lavendar bush which had been the traditional hiding-place of Whisky, Tetanus, Charity, and Fred in succession. Cats have their habits and histories, just the same as humans.

So sometimes, on a working morning, I'd be at my wits' end, almost on the point of going across the town to our ex-neighbours, ringing their bell, and saying. 'Please can Fred come and play?' Specially on a rainy, uninviting day when Taffy was pacing gloomily about the house with drooping head and switching tail, grumbling about the weather and the lack of company, and blaming me for both.

Humblepuppy's arrival changed all that.

At first Taffy considered it necessary to police him, and that kept him fully occupied for hours. He'd sit on guard by the deed-box till Humblepuppy woke up in the morning, and then he'd follow officiously all over the house, wherever the visitor went. Humblepuppy was slow and cautious in his explorations, but by degrees he picked up courage and found his way into every corner. He never once made a puddle; he learned to use Taffy's cat-flap and go out into the garden, though he was always more timid outside and would scamper for home at any loud noise. Planes

225

and cars terrified him, he never became used to them; which made me still more certain that he had been in that deed-box for a long, long time, since before such things were invented.

Presently he learned, or Taffy taught him, to hide in the lavender bush like Whisky, Charity, Tetanus, and Fred; and the two of them used to play their own ghostly version of touch-last for hours on end while I got on with my typing.

When visitors came, Humblepuppy always retired to his deed-box; he was decidedly scared of strangers; which made his behaviour with Mr Manningham, the new rector of Riverland, all the more surprising.

I was dying to learn anything I could of the old rectory's history, so I'd invited Mr Manningham to tea.

He was a thin, gentle, quiet man, who had done missionary work in the Far East and fell ill and had to come back to England. He seemed a little sad and lonely; said he still missed his Far East friends and work. I liked him. He told me that for a large part of the nineteenth century the Riverland living had belonged to a parson called Swannett, the Reverend Timothy Swannett, who lived to a great age and had ten children.

'He was a great-uncle of mine, as a matter of fact. But why do you want to know all this?' Mr Manningham asked. His long thin arm hung over the side of his chair; absently he moved his hand sideways and remarked, 'I didn't notice that you had a puppy.' Then he looked down and said, 'Oh!'

'He's never come out for a stranger before,' I said.

Taffy, who maintains a civil reserve with visitors, sat motionless on the night storage heater, eyes slitted, sphinx-like.

Humblepuppy climbed invisibly on to Mr Manningham's lap.

We agreed that the new rector probably carried a familiar smell of his rectory with him; or possibly he reminded Humblepuppy of his great-uncle, the Revd Swannett.

Anyway, after that, Humblepuppy always came scampering joyfully out if Mr Manningham dropped in to tea, so of course I thought of the rector when summer holiday time came round.

During the summer holidays we lend our house and cat to a lady publisher and her mother who are devoted to cats and think it a privilege to look after Taffy and spoil him. He is always amazingly overweight when we get back. But the old lady has an allergy to dogs, and is frightened of them too; it was plainly out of the question that she should be expected to share her summer holiday with the ghost of a puppy.

So I asked Mr Manningham if he'd be prepared to take Humblepuppy as a boarder, since it didn't seem a case for the usual kind of boarding-kennels; he said he'd be delighted.

I drove Humblepuppy out to Riverland in his deed-box; he was rather miserable on the drive, but luckily it is not far. Mr Manningham came out into the garden to meet us. We put the box down on the lawn and opened it.

I've never heard a puppy so wildly excited. Often I'd been sorry that I couldn't see Humblepuppy, but I was never sorrier than on that afternoon, as we heard him rushing from tree to familiar tree, barking joyously, dashing through the orchard grass – you could see it divide as he whizzed along – coming back to bounce up against us, all damp and earthy and smelling of leaves.

'He's going to be happy with you, all right,' I said, and Mr Manningham's grey, lined face crinkled into its thoughtful smile as he said, 'It's the place more than me, I think.'

Well, it was both of them, really.

After the holiday, I went to collect Humblepuppy, leaving Taffy haughty and stand-offish, sniffing our cases. It always takes him a long time to forgive us for going away.

Mr Manningham had a bit of a cold and was sitting by the fire in his study, wrapped in a Shetland rug. Humblepuppy was on his knee. I could hear the little dog's tail thump against the arm of the chair when I walked in, but he didn't get down to greet me. He stayed in Mr Manningham's lap.

'So you've come to take back my boarder,' Mr Manningham said.

There was nothing in the least strained about his voice or smile but – I just hadn't the heart to take back Humblepuppy. I put my hand down, found his soft wrinkly forehead, rumpled it a bit, and said,

'Well – I was sort of wondering: our spoilt old cat seems to have got used to being on his own again; I was wondering – by any chance – if you'd feel like keeping him?'

Mr Manningham's face lit up. He didn't speak for a minute; then he put a gentle hand down to find the small head, and rubbed a finger along Humblepuppy's chin.

'Well,' he said. He cleared his throat. 'Of course, if you're *quite* sure –'

'Quite sure.' My throat needed clearing too.

'I hope you won't catch my cold.' Mr Manningham said. I shook my head and said. 'I'll drop in to see if you're better in a day or two,' and went off and left them together.

Poor Taffy was pretty glum over the loss of his playmate for several weeks; we had two hours' purgatory every morning after breakfast while he hunted for Humblepuppy high and low. But gradually the memory faded and, thank goodness, now he has found a new friend, Little Grey Furry, a nephew, cousin or other relative of Charity and Fred. Little Grey Furry has learned to play hide-and-seek in the lavender bush, and to use our cat-flap, and clean up whatever's in Taffy's food bowl, so all is well in that department.

But I still miss Humblepuppy. I miss his cold nose exploring the palm of my hand, as I sit thinking, in the middle of a page, and his warm weight leaning against my knee as he watches the commercials. And the scritch-scratch of his toe-nails on the dining-room floor and the flump, flump, as he comes downstairs, and the small hollow in a cushion as he settles down with a sigh.

Oh well. I'll get over it, just as Taffy has. But I was wondering about putting an ad into *Our Dogs* or *Pets' Monthly*: Wanted, ghost of mongrel puppy. Warm welcome, loving home. Any reasonable price paid.

It might be worth a try.

Bang, Bang – Who's Dead?

JANE GARDAM

There is an old house in Kent not far from the sea where a little ghost girl plays in the garden. She wears the same clothes winter and summer – long black stockings, a white dress with a pinafore, and her hair flying about without a hat, but she never seems either hot or cold. They say she was a child of the house who was run over at the drive gates, for the road outside is on an upward bend as you come to the gates of The Elms – that's the name of the house, The Elms – and very dangerous. But there were no motor cars when children wore clothes like that and so the story must be rubbish.

No grown person has even seen the child. Only other children see her. For over fifty years, when children have visited this garden and gone off to play in it, down the avenue of trees, into the walled rose-garden, or down deep under the high dark caves of the polished shrubs where queer things scutter and

scrattle about on quick legs and eyes look out at you from round corners, and pheasants send up great alarm calls like rattles, and whirr off out of the wet hard bracken right under your nose, 'Where've you been?' they get asked when they get back to the house.

'Playing with that girl in the garden.'

'What girl? There's no girl here. This house has no children in it.'

'Yes it has. There's a girl in the garden. She can't half run.'

When last year The Elms came up for sale, two parents – the parents of a girl called Fran – looked at each other with a great longing gaze. The Elms.

'We could never afford it.'

'I don't know. It's in poor condition. We might. They daren't ask much for such an overgrown place.'

'All that garden. We'd never be able to manage it. And the house is so far from anywhere.'

'It's mostly woodland. It looks after itself.'

'Don't you believe it. Those elms would all have to come down for a start. They're diseased. There's masses of replanting and clearing to do. And think of the upkeep of that long drive.'

'It's a beautiful house. And not really a huge one.'

'And would you *want* to live in a house with –'

They both looked at Fran who had never heard of the house. 'With what?' she asked.

'Is it haunted?' she asked. She knew things before you ever said them. Almost before you thought of them.

'Of course not,' said her father.

'Yes,' said her mother.

Fran gave a squealing shudder.

'Now you've done it,' said her father. 'No point now in even going to look at it.'

'How is it haunted?' asked Fran.

'It's only the garden,' said her mother. 'And very *nicely* haunted. By a girl about your age in black stockings and a pinafore.'

'What's a pinafore?'

'Apron.'

'*Apron*. How cruddy.'

'She's from the olden days.'

'Fuddy-duddy-cruddy,' said Fran, preening herself about in her T-shirt and jeans.

After a while though she noticed that her parents were still rattling on about The Elms. There would be spurts of talks and then long silences. They would stand for ages moving things pointlessly about on the kitchen table, drying up the same plate three times. Gazing out of windows. In the middle of Fran telling them something about her life at school they would say suddenly, 'Rats. I expect it's overrun with rats.'

Or, 'What about the roof?'

Or, 'I expect some millionaire will buy it for a Country Club. Oh, it's far beyond us, you know.'

'When are we going to look at it?' asked Fran after several days of this, and both parents turned to her with faraway eyes.

'I want to see this girl in the garden,' said Fran,

because it was a bright sunny morning and the radio was playing loud and children not of the olden days were in the street outside, hurling themselves about on bikes and wearing jeans and T-shirts like her own and shouting out, 'Bang, bang – you're dead.'

'Well, I suppose we could just telephone,' said her mother. 'Make an appointment.'

Then electricity went flying about the kitchen and her father began to sing.

They stopped the car for a moment inside the propped-back iron gates where there stood a rickety table with a box on it labelled 'Entrance Fee. One Pound.'

'We don't pay an entrance fee,' said Fran's father. 'We're here on business.'

'When I came here as a child,' said Fran's mother, 'We always threw some money in.'

'Did you often come?'

'Oh, once or twice. Well yes. Quite often. Whenever we had visitors we always brought them to The Elms. We used to tell them about –'

'Oh yes. Ha ha. The ghost.'

'Well, it was just something to *do* with people. On a visit. I'd not be surprised if the people in the house made up the ghost just to get people to come.'

The car ground along the silent drive. The drive curved round and round. Along and along. A young deer leapt from one side of it to the other in the green shadow, its eyes like lighted grapes. Water in a pool in front of the house came into view.

The house held light from the water. It was a long, low, creamy-coloured house covered with trellis and on the trellis pale wisteria, pale clematis, large papery early roses. A huge man was staring from the ground floor window.

'Is that the ghost?' asked Fran.

Her father sagely, solemnly parked the car. The air in the garden for a moment seemed to stir, the colours to fade. Fran's mother looked up at the gentle old house.

'Oh – look,' she said, 'It's a portrait. Of a man. He seems to be looking out. It's just a painting, for goodness sake.'

But the face of the long-dead seventeenth-century man eyed the terrace, the semicircular flight of steps, the family of three looking up at him beside their motor car.

'It's just a painting.'

'Do we ring the bell? At the front door?'

The half-glazed inner front door above the staircase of stone seemed the door of another shadowy world.

'I don't want to go in,' said Fran. 'I'll stay here.'

'Look, if we're going to buy this house,' said her father, 'You must come and look at it.'

'I want to go in the garden,' said Fran. 'Anyone can see the house is going to be all right.'

All three surveyed the pretty house. Along the top floor of it were heavily-barred windows.

'They barred the windows long ago,' said Fran's mother, 'to stop the children falling out. The children

lived upstairs. Every evening they were allowed to
come down and see their parents for half an hour and
then they went back up there to bed. It was the
custom for children.'

'Did the ghost girl do that?'

'Don't be ridiculous,' said Fran's father.

'But did she?'

'What ghost girl?' said Fran's father. 'Shut up and
come and let's look at the house.'

A man and a woman were standing at the end of the
hall as the family rang the bell. They were there
waiting, looking rather vague and thin. Fran could
feel a sadness and anxiety through the glass of the
wide, high door, the woman with her gaunt old face
just standing; the man blinking.

In the beautiful stone hall at the foot of the stairs
the owners and the parents and Fran confronted each
other. Then the four grown people advanced with
their hands outstretched, like some dance.

'The house has always been in my family,' said the
woman. 'For two hundred years.'

'Can I go out?' asked Fran.

'For over fifty years it was in the possession of three
sisters. My three great-aunts.'

'Mum – can I? I'll stay by the car.'

'They never married. They adored the house. They
scarcely ever left it or had people to stay. There were
never any children in this house.'

'Mum –'

'*Do*,' said the woman to Fran. 'Do go and look around the garden. Perfectly safe. Far from the road.'

The four adults walked away down the stone passage. A door to the dining-room was opened. 'This,' said the woman, 'Is said to be the most beautiful dining-room in Kent.

'What was that?' asked Fran's mother. 'Where is Fran?'

But Fran seemed happy. All four watched her in her white T-shirt running across the grass. They watched her through the dining-room window all decorated round with frills and garlands of wisteria. 'What a sweet girl,' said the woman. The man cleared his throat and went wandering away.

'I think it's because there have never been any children in this house that it's in such beautiful condition,' said the woman. 'Nobody has even been unkind to it.'

'I wouldn't say,' said Fran's mother, 'that children were –'

'Oh, but you can tell a house where children have taken charge. Now your dear little girl would never –'

The parents were taken into a room that smelled of rose-petals. A cherry-wood fire was burning although the day was very hot. Most of the fire was soft white ash. Somebody had been doing some needlework. Dogs slept quietly on a rug. 'Oh, Fran would love –' said Fran's mother looking out of the window again. But Fran was not to be seen.

'Big family?' asked the old man suddenly.

'No. Just – Just one daughter, Fran.'

'Big house for just one child.'

'But you said there had never been children in this house.'

'Oh – wouldn't say never. Wouldn't say never.'

Fran had wandered away towards the garden but then had come in again to the stone hall, where she stopped to look at herself in a long dim glass. There was a blue jar with a lid on a low table, and she lifted the lid and saw a heap of dried rose-petals. The lid dropped back rather hard and wobbled on the jar as if to fall off. 'Children are unkind to houses.' She heard the floating voice of the woman shepherding her parents from one room to another. Fran pulled an unkind face at the jar. She turned a corner of the hall and saw the staircase sweeping upwards and round a corner. On the landing someone seemed to be standing, but then as she looked seemed not to be there after all. 'Oh yes,' she heard the woman's voice, 'Oh yes, I suppose so. Lovely for children. The old nurseries should be very adequate. We never go up there.'

'If there are nurseries,' said Fran's father, 'there must once have been children.'

'I suppose so. Once. It's not a thing we ever think about.'

'But if it has always been in your family it must have been inherited by children?'

'Oh cousins. Generally cousins inherited. Quite

239

strange how children have not been actually born here.' Fran, who was sitting outside on the steps now in front of the open door, heard the little group clatter off along the stone pavement to the kitchens and thought, 'Why are they going on about children so?'

She thought, 'When they come back I'll go with them. I'll ask to see that painted man down the passage. I'd rather be with Mum to see him close.'

Silence had fallen. The house behind her was still, the garden in front of her stiller. It was the moment in an English early summer afternoon when there is a pause for sleep. Even the birds stop singing. Tired by their almost non-stop territorial squawks and cheeps and trills since dawn, they declare a truce and sit still upon branches, stand with heads cocked listening, scamper now and then in the bushes across dead leaves. When Fran listened very hard she thought she could just hear the swish of the road, or perhaps the sea. The smell of the early roses was very strong. Somewhere upstairs a window was opened and a light voice came and went as people moved from room to room. 'Must have gone up the back stairs,' Fran thought and leaned her head against the fluted column of the portico. It was strange. She felt she knew what the house looked like upstairs. Had she been upstairs yet or was she still thinking of going? Going. Going to sleep. Silly.

She jumped up and said, 'You can't catch me. Bang, bang – you're dead.'

She didn't know what she meant by it so she said it again out loud. 'Bang, bang – you're dead.'

She looked at the garden, all the way round from her left to her right. Nothing stirred. Not from the point where a high wall stood with a flint arch in it, not on the circular terrace with the round pond, not in the circle of green with the round gap in it where the courtyard opened to the long drive, and where their car was standing. The car made her feel safe.

Slowly round went her look, right across to where the stone urns on the right showed a mossy path behind them. Along the path, out of the shadow of the house, the sun was blazing and you could see bright flowers.

Fran walked to the other side of the round pond and looked up at the house from the courtyard and saw the portrait again looking at her. It must be hanging in a very narrow passage, she thought, to be so near to the glass. The man was in some sort of uniform. You could see gold on his shoulders and lace on his cuffs. You could see long curls falling over his shoulders. Fancy soldiers with long curls hanging over their uniform! Think of the dandruff.

'Olden days,' said Fran. 'Bang, bang you're dead,' and she set off at a run between the stone urns and into the flower garden. 'I'll run right round the house,' she thought. 'I'll run like mad. Then I'll say I've been all round the garden by myself, and not seen the ghost.'

She ran like the wind all round, leaping the flower-beds, tearing along a showering rose-border, here and there, up and down, flying through another door in a stone wall among greenhouses and sheds and old stables, out again past a rose-red dove-house with the doves like fat pearls set in some of the little holes, and others stepping about the grass. Non-stop, non-stop she ran, across the lawn, right turn through a yew hedge, through the flint arch at last and back to the courtyard. 'Oh yes,' she would say to her friends on their bikes. 'I did. I've been there. I've been all round the garden by myself and I didn't see a living soul.'

'A *living* soul.'

'I didn't see any ghost. Never even thought of one.'

'You're brave, Fran. I'd never be brave like that. Are your parents going to buy the house?'

'Don't suppose so. It's very boring. They've never had any children in it. Like an old-folks' home. Not even haunted.'

Picking a draggle of purple wisteria off the courtyard wall – and pulling rather a big trail of it down as she did so – Fran began to do the next brave thing: to *walk* round the house. Slowly. She pulled a few petals off the wisteria and gave a carefree sort of wave at the portrait in the window. In front of it, looking out of the window, stood a little girl.

Then she was gone.

For less than a flick of a second Fran went cold round the back of the neck. Then hot.

Then she realized she must be going loopy. The girl hadn't been in a pinafore and frilly dress, with long loose hair. She'd been in a white T-shirt like Fran's own. She had been Fran's own reflection for a moment in the glass of the portrait.

'Stupid. Loopy,' said Fran, picking off petals and scattering them down the mossy path, then along the rosy flagstones of the rose garden. Her heart was beating very hard. It was almost pleasant, the fright and then the relief coming so close together.

'Well, I thought I saw the ghost but it was only myself reflected in a window,' she'd say to the friends in the road at home.

'Oh Fran, you are brave.'

'How d'you know it was you? Did you see its face? Everyone wears T-shirts.'

'Oh, I expect it was me all right. They said there'd never been any children in the house.'

'What a cruddy house. I'll bet it's not true. I'll bet there's a girl they're keeping in there somewhere. Behind those bars. I bet she's being imprisoned. I bet they're kidnappers.'

'They wouldn't be showing people over the house and trying to sell it if they were kidnappers. Not while the kidnapping was actually going on, anyway. No, you can tell —' Fran was explaining away, pulling off the petals. 'There wasn't anyone there but me.' She looked up at the windows in the stable-block she was passing. They were partly covered with creeper, but one of them stood open and a girl in a T-shirt was sitting in it, watching Fran.

This time she didn't vanish. Her shiny short hair and white shirt shone out clear. Across her humped-up knees lay a comic. She was very much the present day.

'It's you again,' she said.

She was so ordinary that Fran's heart did not begin to thump at all. She thought, 'It must be the gardener's daughter. They must live over the stables and she's just been in the house. I'll bet she wasn't meant to. That's why she ducked away.'

'I saw you in the house,' Fran said. 'I thought you were a reflection of me.'

'Reflection?'

'In the picture.'

The girl looked disdainful. 'When you've been in the house as long as I have,' she said, 'let's hope you'll know a bit more. Oil paintings don't give off reflections. They're not covered in glass.'

'We won't be keeping the oil paintings,' said Fran grandly. 'I'm not interested in things like that.'

'I wasn't at first,' said the girl. 'D'you want to come up? You can climb over the creeper if you like. It's cool up here.'

'No thanks. We'll have to go soon. They'll wonder where I am when they see I'm not waiting by the car.'

'Car?' said the girl. 'Did you come in a car?'

'Of course we came in a car.' She felt furious suddenly. The girl was looking at her oddly, maybe as if she wasn't rich enough to have a car. Just because she lived at The Elms. And she was only the gardener's daughter anyway. Who did she think she was?

'Well take care on the turn-out to the road then. It's a dangerous curve. It's much too hot to go driving today.'

'I'm not hot,' said Fran.

'You ought to be,' said the girl in the T-shirt, 'with all that hair and those awful black stockings.'

Uninvited Ghosts

PENELOPE LIVELY

Marian and Simon were sent to bed early on the day that the Brown family moved house. By then everyone had lost their temper with everyone else; the cat had been sick on the sitting-room carpet; the dog had run away twice. If you have ever moved you will know what kind of a day it had been. Packing cases and newspaper all over the place . . . sandwiches instead of proper meals . . . the kettle lost and a wardrobe stuck on the stairs and Mrs Brown's favourite vase broken. There was bread and baked beans for supper, the television wouldn't work and the water wasn't hot so when all was said and done the children didn't object too violently to being packed off to bed. They'd had enough, too. They had one last argument about who was going to sleep by the window, put on their pyjamas, got into bed, switched the lights out . . . and it was at that point that the ghost came out of the bottom drawer of the chest of drawers.

It oozed out, a grey cloudy shape about three feet long, smelling faintly of wood-smoke, sat down on a chair and began to hum to itself. It looked like a bundle of bedclothes, except that it was not solid: you could see, quite clearly, the cushion on the chair beneath it.

Marian gave a shriek. 'That's a ghost!'

'Oh, be quiet, dear, do,' said the ghost. 'That noise goes right through my head. And it's not nice to call people names.' It took out a ball of wool and some needles and began to knit.

What would you have done? Well, yes – Simon and Marian did just that and I dare say you can imagine what happened. You try telling your mother that you can't get to sleep because there's a ghost sitting in the room clacking its knitting-needles and humming. Mrs Brown said the kind of things she could be expected to say and the ghost continued sitting there knitting and humming and Mrs Brown went out, banging the door and saying threatening things about if there's so much as another word from either of you . . .

'She can't see it,' said Marian to Simon.

''Course not, dear,' said the ghost. 'It's the kiddies I'm here for. Love kiddies, I do. We're going to be ever such friends.'

'Go away!' yelled Simon. 'This is our house now!'

'No it isn't,' said the ghost smugly. 'Always been here, I have. A hundred years and more. Seen plenty of families come and go, I have. Go to bye-byes now, there's good children.'

The children glared at it and buried themselves under the bedclothes. And, eventually, slept.

The next night it was there again. This time it was smoking a long white pipe and reading a newspaper dated 1842. Beside it was a second grey cloudy shape. 'Hello, dearies,' said the ghost. 'Say how do you do to my Auntie Edna.'

'She can't come here too,' wailed Marian.

'Oh yes she can,' said the ghost. 'Always comes here in August, does Auntie. She likes a change.'

Auntie Edna was even worse, if possible. She sucked peppermint drops that smelled so strong that Mrs Brown, when she came to kiss the children good night, looked suspiciously under their pillows. She also sang hymns in a loud squeaky voice. The children lay there groaning and the ghosts sang and rustled the newspapers and ate peppermints.

The next night there were three of them. 'Meet Uncle Charlie!' said the first ghost. The children groaned.

'And Jip,' said the ghost. 'Here, Jip, good dog – come and say hello to the kiddies, then.' A large grey dog that you could see straight through came out from under the bed, wagging its tail. The cat, who had been curled up beside Marian's feet (it was supposed to sleep in the kitchen, but there are always ways for a resourceful cat to get what it wants), gave a howl and shot on top of the wardrobe, where it sat spitting. The dog lay down in the middle of the rug and set about scratching itself vigorously; evidently it had ghost fleas, too.

Uncle Charlie was unbearable. He had a loud cough that kept going off like a machine-gun and he told the longest most pointless stories the children had ever heard. He said he too loved kiddies and he knew kiddies loved stories. In the middle of the seventh story the children went to sleep out of sheer boredom.

The following week the ghosts left the bedroom and were to be found all over the house. The children had no peace at all. They'd be quietly doing their homework and all of a sudden Auntie Edna would be breathing down their necks reciting arithmetic tables. The original ghost took to sitting on top of the television with his legs in front of the picture. Uncle Charlie told his stories all through the best programmes and the dog lay permanently at the top of the stairs. The Browns' cat became quite hysterical, refused to eat and went to live on the top shelf of the kitchen dresser.

Something had to be done. Marian and Simon also were beginning to show the effects; their mother decided they looked peaky and bought an appalling sticky brown vitamin medicine from the chemists to strengthen them. 'It's the ghosts!' wailed the children. 'We don't need vitamins!' Their mother said severely that she didn't want to hear another word of this silly nonsense about ghosts. Auntie Edna, who was sitting smirking on the other side of the kitchen table at that very moment, nodded vigorously and took out a packet of humbugs which she sucked noisily.

'We've got to get them to go and live somewhere

else,' said Marian. But where, that was the problem, and how? It was then that they had a bright idea. On Sunday the Browns were all going to see their uncle who was rather rich and lived alone in a big house with thick carpets everywhere and empty rooms and the biggest colour television you ever saw. Plenty of room for ghosts.

They were very cunning. They suggested to the ghosts that they might like a drive in the country. The ghosts said at first that they were quite comfortable where they were, thank you, and they didn't fancy these newfangled motor cars, not at their time of life. But then Auntie Edna remembered that she liked looking at the pretty flowers and the trees and finally they agreed to give it a try. They sat in a row on the back shelf of the car. Mrs Brown kept asking why there was such a strong smell of peppermint and Mr Brown kept roaring at Simon and Marian to keep still while he was driving. The fact was that the ghosts were shoving them; it was like being nudged by three cold damp flannels. And the ghost dog, who had come along too of course, was carsick.

When they got to Uncle Dick's the ghosts came in and had a look round. They liked the expensive carpets and the enormous television. They slid in and out of the wardrobes and walked through the doors and the walls and sent Uncle Dick's budgerigars into a decline from which they have never recovered. Nice place, they said, nice and comfy.

'Why not stay here?' said Simon, in an offhand tone.

'Couldn't do that,' said the ghosts firmly. 'No kiddies. Dull. We like a place with a bit of life to it.' And they piled back into the car and sang hymns all the way home to the Browns' house. They also ate toast. There were real toast-crumbs on the floor and the children got the blame.

Simon and Marian were in despair. The ruder they were to the ghosts the more the ghosts liked it. 'Cheeky!' they said indulgently. 'What a cheeky little pair of kiddies! There now . . . come and give uncle a kiss.' The children weren't even safe in the bath. One or other of the ghosts would come and sit on the taps and talk to them. Uncle Charlie had produced a mouth-organ and played the same tune over and over again; it was quite excruciating. The children went around with their hands over their ears. Mrs Brown took them to the doctor to find out if there was something wrong with their hearing. The children knew better than to say anything to the doctor about the ghosts. It was pointless saying anything to anyone.

I don't know what would have happened if Mrs Brown hadn't happened to make friends with Mrs Walker from down the road. Mrs Walker had twin babies, and one day she brought the babies along for tea.

Now one baby is bad enough. Two babies are trouble in a big way. These babies created pandemonium. When they weren't both howling they were crawling around the floor pulling the table-cloths off the tables or hitting their heads on the chairs and hauling the books out of the bookcases. They threw their food all over the kitchen and flung cups of milk on the floor. Their mother mopped up after them and every time she tried to have a conversation with Mrs Brown the babies bawled in chorus so that no one could hear a word.

In the middle of this the ghosts appeared. One baby was yelling its head off and the other was gluing pieces of chewed up bread on to the front of the television. The ghosts swooped down on them with happy cries. 'Oh!' they trilled. 'Bless their little hearts then, diddums, give auntie a smile then.' And the babies stopped in mid-howl and gazed at the ghosts. The ghosts cooed at the babies and the babies cooed at the ghosts. The ghosts chattered to the babies and sang them songs and the babies chattered back and were as good as gold for the next hour and their mother had the first proper conversation she'd had in weeks. When they went the ghosts stood in a row at the window, waving.

Simon and Marian knew when to seize an opportunity. That evening they had a talk with the ghosts. At first the ghosts raised objections. They didn't fancy the idea of moving, they said; you got set in your ways, at their age; Auntie Edna reckoned a strange house would be the death of her.

The children talked about the babies, relentlessly.

And the next day they led the ghosts down the road, followed by the ghost dog, and into the Walkers' house. Mrs Walker doesn't know to this day why the babies, who had been screaming for the last half hour, suddenly stopped and broke into great smiles. And she has never understood why, from that day forth, the babies became the most tranquil, quiet, amiable babies in the area. The ghosts kept the babies amused from morning to night. The babies thrived; the ghosts were happy; the ghost dog, who was actually a bitch, settled down so well that she had puppies which is one of the most surprising aspects of the whole business. The Brown children heaved a sigh of relief and got back to normal life. The babies, though, I have to tell you, grew up somewhat peculiar.

Acknowledgements

The editor and publishers gratefully acknowledge the following for permission to reproduce copyright stories in this book:

'Humblepuppy' by Joan Aiken from *A Harp of Fishbones* published by Jonathan Cape, copyright © Joan Aiken 1972, reprinted by permission of A. M. Heath & Co. Ltd; 'The Veldt' by Ray Bradbury from *The Stories of Ray Bradbury*, copyright © Ray Bradbury 1950, renewed 1977 by Ray Bradbury, reprinted by permission of Grafton Books, a division of HarperCollins Publishers Ltd, and Don Congdon Associates Inc.; 'Hi! It's Me' by Marjorie Darke from *Outsiders* edited by Bryant Newman and published by Collins, copyright © Marjorie Darke 1985, reprinted by permission of Rogers, Coleridge & White Ltd; 'The Spring' by Peter Dickinson from *Beware, Beware* compiled by Jean Richardson and published by Hamish Hamilton, copyright © Peter Dickinson 1987, reprinted by permission of the author; 'Bang, Bang – Who's Dead?' by Jane Gardam from *Beware, Beware* compiled by Jean Richardson and published by Hamish Hamilton, copyright © Jane Gardam 1987, reprinted by permission of David

Higham Associates Limited; 'Spring-heeled Jack' by Gwen Grant from *Book of Sinister Stories* edited by Jean Russell, copyright © Gwen Grant 1982, reprinted by permission of Methuen Children's Books; 'The Passing of Puddy' by Gene Kemp from *Book of Sinister Stories* edited by Jean Russell, copyright © Gene Kemp 1982, reprinted by permission of Methuen Children's Books; 'Uninvited Ghosts' by Penelope Lively from *Frank and Polly Muir's Big Dipper,* copyright © Penelope Lively 1981, reprinted by permission of William Heinemann Ltd; 'The Giant's Necklace' by Michael Morpurgo from *The White Horse of Zennor* edited by Michael Morpurgo, copyright © Michael Morpurgo 1982, reprinted by permission of Kaye & Ward Ltd; 'The Shadow-Cage' by Philippa Pearce from *The Shadow-Cage and Other Tales of the Supernatural* published by Kestrel Books, copyright © Philippa Pearce 1977, reprinted by permission of Puffin Books; 'Goosey Goosey Gander' by Ann Pilling from *Streets Ahead* edited by Valerie Bierman, copyright © Ann Pilling 1989, reprinted by permission of Methuen Children's Books; 'The Horn' by Susan Price from *Here Lies Price*, copyright © Susan Price 1987, reprinted by permission of Faber and Faber Ltd; 'The Men in the Turnip Field' from *Forgotten Folk Tales of the English Counties* by Ruth Tongue, copyright © Ruth Tongue 1970, reprinted by permission of Routledge; 'Almost a Ghost Story' by Robert Westall from *The Haunting of Chas McGill and Other Stories*, copyright © Robert Westall 1983, reprinted by permission of Pan/Macmillan Children's Books; 'A Ghost of One's Own' by Ursula Moray Williams from *The Cat Flap and the Apple Pie and Other Funny Stories* compiled by Lance Salway and published by W. H. Allen, copyright © Ursula Moray Williams 1979, reprinted by permission of Curtis Brown on behalf of the author.